Trapped with Temptation

Elsa Hughes

Contents

Prologue

Five Years Ago

Bodies slick with sweat and greedy with need, their mouths met and devoured. He wanted her, he'd wanted her all night and had watched her hips sway with song and tune in the lively bar tucked into the French Quarter. He could still hear the drums beating to the jazzy rhythm, intense and full of power, floating up to his second floor hotel room.

Or maybe the music was just in his head.

From the moment he'd seen her—hair a fiery and loose tangle of red, eyes a flickering hazel, changing with every new angle of light—he'd been mesmerized. Her body was pliant under his hands now, just as it had been wickedly and fascinatingly full of life and spirit when he'd watched her dance in the bar they'd just met in.

"Now," she whispered, her breath skimming along his stomach muscles that went tout under her touch.

His eyes, alive with adventure, followed her movements as she straddled him, lifted her dress above her head and tossed it away into the thick New Orleans air. There she raised, all flesh and flame, naked.

"I want you now."

Happy to give into the woman's demands, his hands reached for hers, clasped, then pulled her down for a kiss, a nibble of her unpainted mouth he wouldn't mind taking his time with—some other time—and drove into her.

With people below, loud and calling to the sticky night, the clashing sounds of songs, and the sultry glow of the seductive street shining onto their bodies as they tangled, the two strangers rode well into abandon.

Her hips were wild on top of him, riding, racing, and he watched with wonder and gratitude as her breath hitched and her body gave into sensations that sent her to the brink of satisfaction.

He turned her over, and with one more hard thrust into the warmth, she shattered beneath him, body releasing, surrendering, as he surrendered with her, releasing all that held him.

Her hair splayed out in a fan of fire on his hotel sheets, and her face, soft and pink from pleasure, smiled.

He stayed connected, stayed inside of her, and she opened her eyes once again revealing the mesmerizing mix of hazy gold, glimmering bronze, and hints of mischievous dark chocolate.

"You feel incredible," she purred. "My body is incredibly happy and this night has made up for the fact that I had to fly for this business trip. In an airplane. Through the sky."

His lips met hers then he rolled onto his back, pulled her petite body to tuck into his. "Makes two of us that have happy bodies. So you hate to fly. Do you travel a lot for business?"

"I... Well... It seems beside the point now but I don't think we should make this personal."

His laugh was one of an amused and contented man.

"I know, sounds ridiculous. I mean personal, like exchange names or talk about business."

"No names, no business talk." He mulled it over and decided that he'd give the woman whatever she wanted, just to see her lips curve in a smile, just to see her eyes enlivened by sex, seduction, and satisfaction as they had been.

"Tonight is for adventure," she declared.

"You're speaking my language."

"Good. Then let's just let it be a mystery." There was a grin in her words, a hint of playfulness and a dose of sleepiness.

All skin and sweat and satisfaction, she closed her eyes and murmured, "Mystery man."

Feeling the gentle breeze from the fan above, she let the mystery lull her into a dream.

Chapter 1

The helicopter swayed in the sky and so did her stomach. It had been enough to fly across the country, which she often did for business, but that was after the proper preparatory measures of peaceful meditation music playing in her ear-buds and drops of a calming homeopathic remedy under her tongue. But the peace and remedy had worn off, and so had the professional polish she'd left California with.

Now, one side of her crisp white collar was popped up, the other laying flat with a smearing of respectable spice colored lipstick pressed into the fabric. She felt awful and couldn't help but show it. As her stomach dipped into another quick tug and low pull followed by a few fast flips, she figured her face was likely as green as the cash she'd stuck in the inside pocket of her purse for tips along the business trip.

Blades chopped at the thick gray opaque clouds that coated the New Hampshire sky. The pilot told her that it wouldn't be too much further and she pressed her lips together to refrain from pointing out that any distance further was too far. But given that in a few hours she'd be back in the same helicopter returning to the airport, she sucked it up and attempted to study the storm that brewed around them but couldn't bring herself to appear as anything other than sick to her stomach rather than confident and professional as she would have liked.

Showing how she felt came with the territory of having red hair, her mother had explained to her as a child. She'd been told it was a privilege, the gift of being an innately colorful person, but as she approached the home of one of the wealthiest entrepreneurs in the country, she cursed it. It would be so much easier to be one of those women who could just remain glossy and perfect at all times, regardless of what was felt on the inside.

Emerson Brown closed her eyes, then opened her eyes, then closed them again. Nothing made her feel better. Except for the thought of strangling Liam Wyatt who'd arranged the tin bug with top wings to pick her up in the first place.

But not even hating an elusive billionaire made her feel less like throwing up.

Don't think about throwing up, she reminded herself. Think about work. Purpose.

There, she decided. Better. She was the Vice President of Business Development for a social media technology start-up and she was great at it. She could certainly fly from San Francisco to Boston to New Hampshire for a meeting like the respectable professional she was.

Except she hadn't planned on the private helicopter ride. She'd been told she'd be picked up at the Boston Logan airport but had assumed a car would be waiting. A car was a lovely, wonderful way to transport a person as it kept all wheels intelligently and practically on the ground.

The initial curiosity she'd felt when the apparently brilliant and secretive business-man's assistant called to set up the meeting with her had dissipated during the rough ride through the sky. But she was a professional, and a fine one at that. She would get the deal done. Of course, to be fair, she didn't know why he'd scheduled the meeting so she didn't actually know what kind of deal he was interested in. She'd done some of her usual due diligence in preparation but even after days of searching, she found very little information on the man or his holdings.

At least her company knew where she was, she decided. Just in case the guy turned out to be some eccentric psychopathic killer. Her CEO had all but begged to come with her, excited to meet the mysterious mogul, but at the last minute had flown to Britain, much to his dismay, to meet with an investor who threatened to pull his money.

The invitation had been to stay the night at Liam Wyatt's camp in New Hampshire, but that sounded quite dreadful and would have kept her away from her son regardless of her personal feelings. Plus she had no interest in brushing her teeth in a tent cabin next to some agoraphobic business beast. No one but her son, Archer, knew the color of her toothbrush these days. That information was much too personal. So she'd shocked her over-eager CEO and agreed to a one-hour meeting only. Then she'd fly back to California and be home in time to kiss her son's head, get a couple hours of sleep, wake up before dawn to bake, then drop him off at daycare with two dozen cupcakes for their little party.

She couldn't, for the life of her, remember what the party was for but she did store every fact and figure pertaining to business in her head and gave herself a pass when it came to remembering reasons for daycare parties.

The life of a working single mom wasn't an easy one, but a rich one nonetheless, and she never considered herself bored.

Thank God her mom lived with them. Always at the ready, her mom treated each one of Emerson's business trips like her own vacation. She got to play with her grandson and give him extra candy, run around and encourage chaotic noise with the rambunctious boy, and sleep in the middle of Emerson's plush bed during overnight trips.

The helicopter dipped in altitude and her stomach lurched right along with it, pushing the wistful smile she'd worked up down her face into a deep frown of pure dread.

She considered death as a viable alternative to business trips.

The pilot announced their arrival at camp and Emerson glanced out the window.

Her mouth dropped and held open in shock as a massive stone castle came into view. It filled the window she stared out of, sprawling with several wings, snuggled up against the shadowy lake with a thick blanket of trees and remnant patches of snow surrounding.

She'd been expecting a tent cabin that required the literal act of camping, not a New England castle with long stretches of rough stone and curved drum towers popping up at various corners and juts. The place looked like it belonged in the United Kingdom, not in the United States.

As they lowered toward the helipad in a wide grass clearing, her brain began to spin in jerky circles along with the beat of the spinning blades. Even with the distraction of shock at the site of the imposing castle, she fought the sensation of losing her wary stomach and watched as her world spun.

When the helicopter finally met with the ground, her full and whirling mind settled long enough to register that she was expected to take the man's hand that held open the door. He motioned for her to stay down, the man in the black tie, as she was gently guided along.

Disoriented as they made their way to what she considered safety, away from the torture machine—otherwise known as a helicopter—she barely registered anything else until the contraption lifted in the air once again and the man in the tie wandered off with her purse and computer bag.

Ground, she was on the ground where she belonged. And she didn't even care if she'd been kidnapped or the fancy man stole her laptop and was on the run. Nothing mattered nearly as much as being on the ground.

Momentum kept her legs walking, one in front of the other, and she dazedly rethought the sharp black leather heels she now wobbled in.

"You look pale. You alright?"

She pulled her focus away from the ground and stopped, scanning up the man's legs that filled out a pair of jeans much too nicely, then gazed further up and over his strong and steady chest to where a blur of sculptured features, dark stubble, and cool gray eyes met with warm brown waves of hair.

Something in her shivered and simultaneously overheated her already frazzled nerves. "You," she managed.

Hair blown into disheveled knots, her collar still out of whack, lipstick printed on her shirt, and her five-foot two-inch frame barely able to balance on her high heels, she provided an easy, remembering smile then gave into the warmth and slid into the gilded glory of relaxation and promptly passed out.

"Where am I?" Emerson sat up from the long leather couch she laid on, a forest green plaid cashmere blanket covering her.

The stone fireplace, tall enough for her to stand in, hissed at her in response.

She stayed still, taking a moment to focus her eyes, and noticed that large wool socks, much too big for her feet, were in the place of her hard earned classic Jimmy Choos.

Windows, too high up to see out of, let in stark white light that reflected down into the massive room.

She rose, wobbled upon standing, then slid along the creaking wood floor, slowly, as her head was still a bit light, and looked around for people. "Hello?"

The memory of seeing a face that was faintly familiar fuzzily came into focus. That had been quite some dream if that's what it'd been. She hadn't thought about that night, that amazing night with that amazing man, in years. And as the memory rolled through her mind, her body warmed in response. He'd been exactly what she needed that night in New Orleans, had fulfilled her body, mind and spirit when she'd been heartbroken and craving a distraction.

Starting down the impressively long stone hall that housed too many knotty pine doors to count, she reminded herself this was a business trip. She would think about sex with that stranger—the only time she'd ever done that, had ever desired that—on her way back to the airport. Maybe if she thought about sex she could survive the impending helicopter ride.

She came across a restroom and absently decided to do a quick mirror check.

Gasping at her reflection—lipstick smeared, hair resembling a matted bird's nest, and now both sides of her collar featuring makeup—she quickly shut the door and locked it.

"Good God, Emerson," she whispered the reprimand.

Dampening a washcloth, she cleaned up the best she could, pulled a hand through her disheveled hair in lieu of a comb, and re-tucked her white button-down shirt into her fitted gray pencil skirt.

That better have been the sexiest groundskeeper she'd ever seen and not the elusive businessman Liam Wyatt she'd fainted in front of, she thought, wincing. But he did, in her hazy pre-fainting memory, look a lot like that man she'd slept with in New Orleans.

Death really was sounding better than business trips.

Cringing, she poked at ideas as to what may have happened while she'd been unconscious. Had he caught her when she'd fallen? Had he carried her into the castle? Taken off her shoes? Slipped a pair of socks on her feet?

She winced again.

At least she'd painted the fresh swipe of fire engine red on her toes before she left, she decided.

She would do her best to put back on the professional face she'd left San Francisco with, get the meeting over with, and get back to her son.

Deciding she'd done a decent enough job putting the pieces of herself back together, she wandered back out into the hall and followed the line of archways. The cave-like hallways made of polished stone featuring domed ceilings were the most interesting to her. With her forever-active imagination, she could see them through her son's eyes, full of wonder and curiosity.

She wished for her phone to text her mom to check on the pair, see how they were getting on, to make sure he wasn't wearing his Superman costume to daycare. Again. Once a week was enough and she'd told Archer that superheroes needed rest.

The sleepless hypocrite in her pushed forward to find Liam Wyatt, get the meeting over with, then get back on the dreaded modes of transport.

A raucous crash interrupted the silence and she wandered toward the sound. One room led into another, intimidatingly formal and somehow still welcomingly open, and she found herself back in the living room.

"Darwin, no."

She turned at the man's command as a Great Dane flopped his weight across the floor and lifted onto his back paws then pushed with his front before she could react.

"Darwin, dammit, no."

Emerson pushed back up to standing as the dog was pulled off of her. Brushing off the frozen mud that now smeared on her dress shirt, she finally got a good look at the man she'd fainted in front of. "It is you."

She watched, studied him as he shoved the lanky dog through the nearest door then pulled it closed. When he turned and their eyes met, her heartbeat roared to life in her chest.

A grin covered his face as he walked toward her. "Emerson."

Her name rolling off his tongue so casually caused her eyebrow to shoot up in question.

"You...you're not surprised to see me? You know my name? I haven't seen you since New Orleans when we..." She took one step back, away from him. "Who are you?"

He stopped just short of reaching her, and his attentive gray eyes scanned her over. When his gaze settled on her face, light revealed the shadowy flecks of danger that sliced through the smoky gray.

"Liam Wyatt. Welcome to camp."

"You're Liam Wyatt?" She stared at him, waiting for explanation. When no other words were spoken, she took another step back, then another, getting closer to the fireplace that danced with flames, shim-mering in colors of bold orange and icy blue.

"Why did you bring me here?"

Chapter 2

Liam rounded toward the wet bar in the corner of the vast living room he'd kept open and sparsely decorated on purpose. He didn't like knick-knacks, had no taste for antiques, but loved open space and natural materials like mismatched stone and authentic, blemished wood. He'd built his very own camp in New Hampshire exactly as he wanted it.

Summers had been spent on the property as kids—him, his sister, his brother, all tossing one another in the lake, hiding in the thick forest, fighting battles with plastic swords and grimy hands. And after too many adult years spent in New York, building his business, discovering new tech companies to invest in, helping them to succeed, he'd been ready to retreat to the woods that were part of his family's roots.

But he couldn't think about family now—he'd been steeped in his brother's illness, fighting for care no matter the cost, offering to build wings in hospitals if it meant his brother would be okay. He hadn't just been steeped in it, he corrected, he'd drowned in it. And hadn't that been why he'd flown in Emerson? To remind him of adventure? To help him forget about the sanitized scent of the hospital and the constant tug of guttural fear?

Pouring brown liquor from a crystal decanter into two glasses, figuring on two fingers of fine brandy, he calmed at the idea she was there, in his home. Finally.

He knew she wondered and waited, and even though he'd been thinking of this moment in flashes over the years, he took the time to collect himself. He hadn't thought through the words, only the desire. Liam lived in the moment and wasn't one to waver in his desires.

And as he'd left the hospital room for a cup of coffee on a sunny day in Boston the week prior, he'd glanced back in and had seen his sister-in-law holding his brother's hand. He hadn't given consideration to why Emerson flashed in his mind at that moment. Instead he just did what he needed to do to get her there.

"It's great to see you, Emerson. You look even more incredible than when I saw you last in New Orleans."

She frowned as she took the drink he handed her. Instead of sipping it, she simply held it in her hand and waited for answers. "What am I doing here? Are you really interested in a partnership with my company? Is this really a meeting?"

He sat back into the couch, the glow of the fire warming the edges of his fierce face, pulling back a drink of brandy that warmed from within. "One could argue we're meeting now."

Temper that came as natural as her red hair bubbled under the surface. "Fine. You're not going to answer my questions, fine. Since you don't at all seem surprised to see me, let me make some assumptions. You somehow found out my name and what? Brought me here thinking we'd repeat what we did in New Orleans years ago? You made me fly across the country and endure a damn helicopter ride—I hate flying, by the way—all to what? Come here just on some sort of whim of yours?"

Fidgety, she set down the glass so she wouldn't be tempted to throw it.

Hands fisted on her hips, she waited for him to respond. When he only looked at her with amusement hinting at his lips, his confident and competent lips, fury clawed.

"You think just because you're some wealthy businessman you can order people around? You can't pluck me out of my life and trick me into going places just because it amuses you, you unscrupulous, arrant butt-face."

His head tilted slightly to the side and he peered up at her as she paced. "Unscrupulous, arrant butt-face? I've been called a lot of things in my life, never heard that before."

A defiant eyebrow lifted once again. "Maybe not to your face."

He smiled and rose from the couch, his body filling the room, kicking up her temper another notch.

As he walked toward her, she stopped and stood her ground in front of the fire, didn't budge this time; there was no stepping back. "I'm not to be bought or messed with. I...can't believe I'm saying this, but I want to get back on that helicopter and I want to get home to California. Now."

Her words and the flames that came with them didn't deter him. He approached until they were face to face, one breath apart.

"You're right to be mad." His voice was calm in its intensity. "I should've told you that I wanted to see you but I didn't know if you'd come. If that night and morning in New Orleans taught me anything, it's that you're a strong-willed woman who knows her mind."

She scowled at him.

"My life's changed a lot in the past five years and I brought you here because, well I hadn't really thought about it like this, but you've been the one constant question through it all. Something about you stuck with me and I wanted to see how you are. How your life is. Every time I think of you, I wonder if you're happy. Then last week I saw your picture in a technology trade article about the expansion of your company and I arranged for you to come here."

Struggling for her breath, for words, her mind spun as it had on the helicopter. Her thoughts, for one hot blaze of a moment, rushed into temptation, into desire to feel him, their bodies touching. But she wasn't the same woman she was years ago. She was a mother and an executive now. She had a mortgage payment, a business to run, and cupcakes to get to her son's daycare.

Sex and adventure with mystery men didn't factor into her life now.

"I have to get home. I'm sorry, I can't be part of this...whatever this is. It's maddening, and flattering a little bit, I suppose, but you could have any woman you want. I have to get home. You should...put your efforts elsewhere."

He'd had other women and didn't want them. He wanted her.

"You slept for quite awhile today."

She rolled her eyes and poked a finger at his chest to push him away. "Great. Thank you so much for the reminder. I told you, if you couldn't tell from my elegant fainting display, I hate flying. So while I may sound like a masochist, please call the helicopter back as I'd like to leave."

He grabbed for her hand and the strength of his grip had a memory playing back in her mind. His hands on her body, gripping, pulling, feeling, gliding.

She tried to tug her hand away but he only held tighter as he pulled her along, through the cavernous hallway into another room with a tall stretch of windows and yet another fireplace.

They stopped at the glass that reached two stories up and stretched wide across. Her mouth gasped open.

"I meant you were out for awhile and the storm rolled in. Helicopter won't be flying anywhere."

Everything was coated white in every direction. At least three feet, if not more, with flakes falling fast from the sky and swirling with the whipping wind. The expanse of the lake was the only clearing but the surface was frosted with ice.

"You planned this."

Now he laughed. "Money doesn't sway Mother Nature, I'm afraid."

"Okay, whatever, it's fine. I'll just drive. Have a car I can borrow to get to Boston?"

"Emerson." His hands laid on her shoulders and he maneuvered her to face him. "No one's driving anywhere in this stuff. Roads and airports are closed."

"No," was all she could think to say. "No. They can't be. I have to get home."

"I'd say you're stuck here for now. I'll turn on the news so you can see for yourself."

"I can see the snow for myself!" she yelled, knowing she was starting to lose that clenched grip on control. She consciously breathed out the mad to a steaming simmer. "I need my phone. Where's my purse? That man with the black tie...that sounds nuts so hopefully I wasn't hallucinating.

Anyway, he took my purse and I need my phone. I need to make a call."

"He works for me but he left for the day to help his daughter with a project for school. Some kind of abstract art deal, hence the black tie. He put your purse in a guest room and I'll get it for you but your phone won't work out here. No reception."

Watching her face set into another storm of mad, he reached for her hand and had her on the move again. "Landline's this way."

"Aren't you one of the wealthiest men in the world or country or something? Why don't you just build a cell-tower so phones work here?"

"Good idea. Want a job?"

"I have a job."

"Want a better one?"

"No. I want a phone that works."

"Almost there," he said as he pushed open double doors to an expansive office overlooking the lake. The desk was broad and curved like wavy lines of the sea, the windows tall and inviting, the computer screen the size of a television.

"Is anything in this place normal sized? Everything is huge."

At his slow side grin, heat filled her body, pink springing to life on her cheeks.

"That was not a reference to...you. Though I suppose it fits. I mean...it fits...really well, actually. Don't know how because you're... and I'm..." She was fumbling and she knew it so she let out a steadying breath. "You're huge, this place is huge, now please leave so I can have the room and make a few calls."

She sat in the chair behind the desk, partly because her legs were beginning to wobble, and partly because doing so helped her feel more in charge of things.

Liam leaned in close and kissed her lips, directly and intently, then lifted and walked out of the room, closing the doors behind him.

He'd been complimented then kicked out of his own office and was completely pleased by the idea.

Chapter 3

Emerson was red in the face and over-heated as she hunted down Liam Wyatt.

Lost in a maze of hallways and wings, she finally caught the scent of something sweet, possibly chocolate, and sped up her pursuit, determined not to let hunger deter her from the fight she had in her.

After many failed attempts at pushing through doors, she finally pummeled through a swinging door and arrived in a kitchen that had long sweeping white marble counters, a center island the size of her entire kitchen, and appliances that looked more like technological inventions than kitchen apparatuses.

"Cookie?" Liam asked, pulling a sheet of chocolate chip cookies from the oven.

"I don't want a damn cookie."

The man was an enigma—simple surrounded by complexity.

"More for me." Overlooking her tone, figuring she'd explain it eventually if she wanted to, he transferred cookies to a plate. "Can I get you something to drink?"

"No," she said sternly, refusing to let go of her bite. "I'm mad at you, and you're going to listen to me. You tricked me into coming here and I don't care to be tricked. My CEO is pissed as hell that you didn't invite me here to talk about a partnership because he's..." she considered her words, "misleadingly intrigued by your business sense, and wanted to do a deal with you."

"Misleadingly intrigued? You mean because no one should be intrigued by an unscrupulous, arrant butt-face?" Unaffected, he bit at a cookie, decided the batter required more nuts.

"This isn't funny, Liam. My CEO is pissed because he thinks I'm not doing my job, which technically he's right. My stomach is still woozy from the ridiculous helicopter ride, my shirt is filthy from your unruly dog, flights are cancelled at least until tomorrow which means that I'm stuck here with you, and my son needs his damn cupcakes!" The eruption of anger finished with some huffs and paces around the kitchen.

Liam mixed more pecans into the bowl followed by a quick, barely perceptible pause.

"You have a son?" He considered the idea as he strong-armed the thick batter.

"I have a son who needs his mother at home. I'm supposed to bake cupcakes and deliver them to daycare tomorrow."

"Do you need a nanny too? Is he being cared for while you're gone?"

"What? What kind of response is that? He's with my mom and is just fine. She's probably happy she gets him all to herself a little longer. What're you doing?"

She watched him pull his phone out, press a couple buttons then hold it to his face while he piled clumps of dough onto a cookie sheet.

"I'm sorry, is my life boring to you?"

"Not in the least," he responded matter-of-factly. "Calling my assistant."

She threw her arms up in the air. "And why does your phone work in here and mine doesn't?"

"I tweaked it."

She huffed out a sigh. The man was infuriating, that was all there was to it. It was simple, he was simple. And complex and arrogant and entitled and manipulative and maddeningly attractive.

"Need you to hunt down some cupcakes and have them delivered. Emerson here will give you the details. Hold on."

He handed his phone over. "Here's April. Just tell her what you need, when you need it, and where it's going."

A wave of parental guilt swamped her. "That's cheating. I'm a mom. I'm supposed to be there to make the cupcakes myself."

"But you can't. Weather. This is next best." He kissed the top of her head as if the act were routine.

She frowned as she relayed the details to the polite and efficient assistant then handed the phone back after noting that it smelled like him—clean, masculine, wealthy, and dangerous.

As if wealth had a smell, but it did, she decided. So did danger. Whatever the scent, it knotted in her stomach as he ended the call then placed a cookie on a small plate and set it in front of her.

Temper deflating, she leaned against the thick slab of marble that covered the island and stared at the cookie.

She wanted to stay mad, because if she considered any other emotion, it would likely be desire. And she didn't want desire, she didn't have time for it and it didn't fit in her life. It wasn't the worst thing in the world to be stuck in the ridiculously named "camp" with an attractive man who baked a batch of cookies, then fixed problems with a single call to his assistant. Nor did it really hurt anything to let desire play in her mind.

As she talked herself in and out of thoughts, knots tugged tight in her stomach and were, she noticed, faintly familiar. The last time she'd felt them had been five years ago in New Orleans with Liam.

Which was a sad state of her love life that the strongest memory of sex and passion was from five years ago, but she just had other more immediately important things in her life now. She was living real life, in the real world, as a single working mother.

Snow fell fast and without sound outside the broad kitchen windows that were foggy around the edges, making life around her feel quiet compared to her thoughts. There weren't any colors except the black of the lake and the white of the snow but it was a pretty picture, stark and somehow cozy.

Why the enormous stone castle kept any heat in it was a mystery to Emerson. And so was the man she'd once had a spontaneous tangle with, who seemed comfortable in every moment he stepped into.

His comfort was altogether unsettling.

She sighed out the last of her temper, for now, and gave in to the cookie.

"Tell me about your son," he said tossing a dash of cinnamon into the bowl for the next batch.

Men didn't want to hear about her child, she knew. She'd dated—if it could be called that—in sparse increments and discovered most men ignored the topic, some inquired, dipping a toe in the water before running the other way, and some went out of their way to be so okay with it that they came across as attempting the façade of not freaking out even though they actually were.

Any way you looked at it, the men she'd dated didn't really want to know about her son so she'd stopped dating.

Not that she was on a date now, she corrected, watching the muscles in Liam's legs move him around the kitchen.

"His name is Archer, he's four, he loves Legos, and he's the love of my life." She sped through the response. "Why are you baking?"

Comfortable with what he considered dual conversations rather than a change of topic, he slid another cookie onto Emerson's plate and thought about what it would be like to have a son, a little being that looked up to him.

It was a thought he'd considered lately more than he ever thought he would, but then again family had occupied him for the past month since his brother's diagnosis. It was the one thing that had escaped him in his success, having a family of his own, and the one thing he found himself missing.

"Legos are amazing. You can create a whole different world that you dominate and rule. Whatever you can dream, you can build. I like cookies so I made some. Thought you'd like them too, given the number of beignets you ate that morning in New Orleans."

The curved lips and knowing sparkle in his eyes buoyed inside of her and she couldn't help but let out a laugh at herself.

"Well, I'd worked up quite an appetite, I suppose."

"We."

"We?"

"We'd worked up an appetite. Ever wonder what would have happened if we'd exchanged names?"

She glanced out the window, her gaze settling on singular flakes, one after the other, as they fell.

"I have an amazing son so I can't answer any what-ifs because I wouldn't trade him for the world, even a hypothetical one."

He slid a bowl into the sink, tossed in some of the utensils he'd used. "Didn't mean it like that."

Liam stopped short. "You said he's four years old?"

She took another bite of the warm cookie, perfectly melted and gooey in the middle. "Yeah, he's an amazing little guy. Anyway, tell me something about you. What have you been up to? Other than living in a castle."

Emerson looked around for somewhere to sit. "You need some stools or chairs in here, by the way."

Liam's mind kicked into gear. He stepped toward her, lifted her up and plopped her on the island to sit, then stayed where he was, standing imposingly close to her. "Emerson."

"Liam." She mockingly matched his serious tone.

"Timing of things sounds suspicious. Anything you want to tell me?"

"Timing of what? Oh, you mean Archer? Wow, no. I'm so sorry. You're not his father. I guess I should've made that clear from the start. Incredibly sorry." She laughed at the panicked look on his face.

"His father is a man I broke up with before you and I...well, yeah...and we briefly got back together after you and I, and we created Archer. That sounds weird. Anyway, he's not in the picture, my ex, and decided he didn't want to even meet Archer."

Liam watched her, listening to every word, watching every fleck of emotion pass on her face as she spoke. "He just abandoned you both?"

Her hand lifted to Liam's chest, a brief companionable touch, a friendly gesture, she told herself. "It wasn't like that. He just didn't want to be part of it. He would have stayed with me out of obligation if I wanted that, but I didn't. A relationship based on obligation isn't something I'm interested in."

"What are you interested in?"

Because she was seated on the cool slab of marble rather than standing at her usual petite height, their faces were close—his gray eyes intent, curious, knowing, his lips waiting.

"I haven't really thought that much about it lately. I ultimately want love...I guess." She glanced out the window again, letting an image roll through her mind.

"I want to see a man I've been with for thirty years across the room and I want to still desire him. And I want to be able to just hold hands through difficult life moments, you know? Someone who's there with you." The gold in her hazel eyes glowed with imagined nostalgia.

"But my friends think I'm crazy to want all that with one person. But anything less is just...not enough. Which explains why I'm single, I guess."

He nudged her face up, just slightly. "It can't be easy to raise a kid on your own and be an executive, working your way to the top. You're still the same fiery, passionate woman I met in New Orleans, but you're softer now too. Like you have this wise softness in the center of you that you keep under the surface. But it's there. And it's beautiful."

Speechless, she reminded herself to breathe. She inhaled, exhaled, and the fringes of the stress from the morning and afternoon relaxed into the warmth of his words.

"I don't know what to say. I've never heard anyone say anything like that. In the movies maybe, but never in real life. Never from anyone who..." She wanted to describe him but words escaped her that would describe the enormity of him, the startling depth of him.

"From anyone who is you," she decided.

He watched her mind work, her breath catch. Desire, swift and strong, pulled hard.

"You should set down that cookie."

"What?" Glancing down, she saw the cookie in her grip. "Oh. Why? I might want to take a bite."

The smile she offered fell, along with the cookie, when he reached behind her and pulled her hips closer to the edge of the marble counter, closer to him.

"Oh," she managed, feeling herself loosing control. She was in charge of details, of deals, of a team, of her household, and now, secluded in a snowy castle with a man who so easily took what he wanted and gave his presence so sincerely, temptation took over.

"Just don't bite me," she whispered, anticipation lighting her eyes, remembering the nibble marks she'd carried home from New Orleans.

"No promises." Liam held her face, met her gaze before his lips met hers in devastatingly slow movements designed with such potency, her mind slipped into the silkiness of it, forgetting all thought, all worry.

"No promises," she repeated, understanding the double meaning. A no-strings-attached, no promises fling that no one had to know about was a luxury she rarely afforded herself. After a quick mental lashing that she was giving him the very thing he'd brought her there for, she decided she was taking what she wanted as well so it was a fair game.

Again, with a slow study of each other, her body opened, warmed, and wanted nothing more than him in that heated winter moment.

Chapter 4

With her still seated on the counter, that's how Liam wanted her, he decided. Of course, he could take her anywhere in the castle, it wouldn't matter. His want was purely for her. It just so happened she was handily in his kitchen.

He didn't desire the quick flick of passion from last time; he wanted to devour her in maddeningly slow bites. But he didn't do well with limitations and knew himself well enough to know he broke rules just as fast as he made them.

Not that he was making rules, as he firmly believed rules were not only made to be broken, but they were made by people who desperately wanted to break them, rendering the act of rule creation utterly ridiculous in the first place.

No rules, no boundaries, no limitations. He simply wanted Emerson Brown.

Up against that thin line of restraint, his lips lingered near hers, playing, teasing, sampling, until her mouth opened. Tongues tasted, finally, desperately, and with an enduring familiarity and fervent curiosity, they each took, each demanded more.

He heard her breath hitch as his fingers slid under the hem of her snug pencil skirt that callously kept her legs tightly together, hugging curves. He could appreciate the skirt and what it did for her incredible figure but wanted it gone.

Slowly, his fingers dragged up the edge to the top of her thighs, his purposeful hands trailing on her silky skin.

Heavy-lidded eyes watched him, he knew it, and he looked at her, ready, and gently guided her legs open.

He had to see her, feel her, touch her.

Sliding the flimsy black lace aside, his body demanded with a drastic ferocity not at all designed for patient nibbling. Nothing short of everything with her would be enough.

"You're even more beautiful than I remember," he murmured at the site of her bare skin, smooth as sin. His thumb glided along and dipped in to find her warm and wet and ready.

Her eyes closed and her head tilted back and he watched with satisfaction as she soaked in the pleasure. He'd remembered that about her and had forgotten how powerful it was, to please a woman who embraced pleasure for the sake of it.

Vital with demand, ready to take, he ripped at the lace and tossed it away.

Her eyes opened, surprise filling her face, and after the briefest of smiles, reached for the buttons of his jeans.

He was huge, just as she remembered him, and filled with just as much potency beneath the quiet confidence. Pulling him out, her fingers feeling along the tip of him, she guided him toward her.

Their bodies touched, hard and soft, skin and heat, meeting just at the surface.

Each of them watched where their bodies joined together, fascinated, enticed by the other.

On a moan, he slid further into her, held her hips as sensations rippled through her. She'd forgotten what it felt like—to desire a man, to be fulfilled by a man. She'd forgotten all of it.

And now, Liam Wyatt was fulfilling her.

Matching her need, meeting her demands, his body, slick with sweaty heat in the dead of winter, glistening in the glow from the reflection of the frozen white won-derland outside, moved in hers.

Feeling the power of having him inside of her, touching her in all the right places, sensations overwhelmed, rippled through, and her body pushed and pulled as she throbbed alive and went flying fast over the edge of all reason.

He held onto her, still gripping, as he dove over, into the wonder with her.

Both breathless, they each stayed where they were—her seated on the counter, him standing in front of her, arms wrapped around each other.

"Next time we take our clothes off," his deep and relaxed voice said.

She laughed, her lips against his neck. "I do need to get back to real life at some point."

"This is real life, Emerson."

The way he said it, the tone, had her fum-bling. "You may do this all the time but I haven't done this in years, so for me, it's not real life."

Defiantly, she tried to scoot away but he caught her soft face in his hands.

"Moments are as real as we make them. So for me, this was one hell of a moment. And I want more of them. With you."

The sincerity of him tripped her, the presence of him overpowered her, and she fought to get back some semblance of a grip on herself.

"Well, I'm here now, aren't I?" Her mouth, pink and plump from kisses, smiled.

His eyebrow raised up, conspiratorially. "Yes, you are. Almost fully clothed, almost naked, and right in front of me. I like you just like this." He frowned. "Well, maybe..."

He lifted her hips and pulled her off the island then yanked at the buttons on her white shirt stained by lipstick and paw prints.

Taking his queue, she unzipped the back of her skirt then moved on to his clothes, dropping them into a puddle on the wood floors.

"Naked. Now this is how I like you."

At her laugh, he lifted both of them on top of the massive marble slap and took her, melted her once again, and reminded her how much she truly loved being a woman.

They both lay sprawled on the considerable island, clothes askew around them, sex and cookies having steamed up the frozen windows.

"Water," she managed.

"Wine," he responded. "You do things to me, Emerson Brown. We celebrate with wine."

Just beats before she sat up, he anticipated her and lifted her onto his body to shield her from the marble that was contrastingly cool under their bodies.

Limbs intertwined in a jumbled heap, mouths met, and moments lingered.

"Wine, dinner, maybe if you're lucky I'll feed you dessert." He dragged his limbs from the tangle, sat up, scooted them both to the edge and decided that he liked how her legs wrapped around him. She was petite and easily held...

"Next time," he muttered as they both found footing on the floor of the kitchen.

"What?"

"Nothing. Like red or white?"

"Is there any color other than red?" She asked, running a hand through her hair that'd gone unruly yet again—this time for reasons better than passing out after flying.

Mouth ripe and ready, he laid a hand on her hip, pulled her in, and planted a kiss on her lips. "Red it is."

He poured generously from a bottle he'd decanted earlier, handed her a glass, and decided he liked her in his kitchen.

She buttoned herself into the collared shirt he'd worn while he pulled on jeans, leaving the top button casually undone.

"Where's your dog, by the way?"

"Who knows. Getting into trouble or guarding the place. One or the other, maybe both. He likes to explore, find adventures. Usually only see him when he's hungry. Pretty independent, that dog."

"Like owner, like dog."

"Not all of us are lucky enough to pass our genes onto a son, like you."

His words were not always personal, he was, after all, notoriously adept at hiding his personal life from the public, but when he spoke, there was meaning in what he said.

"You want kids?"

"Hadn't thought much about it until recently."

She sipped her wine. "Is that a yes?"

He sniffed his wine without taking a drink. Instead he held his glass and looked through the misted window toward the woods he'd built countless forts in as a kid, imagined that for his own. The joy, the scratches, the scars, the adventure. After a long and silent lull, he said, "Yes."

Her full laugh echoed in the kitchen. "Men get so weird about the topic of kids. You're a strange lot. You act as though a baby could fall from the sky at any moment and land in your lap."

"The thought is just new for me, so it's nothing I've ever talked about," he said calmly.

Her head tilted, eyeing him. "What changed?"

A text dinged through on his phone and he pulled it out to read.

Topic over, she could take the hint.

She sipped at her wine again, sampled, and decided that even after drinking cheap wine at home and expensive wine at business dinners, she couldn't tell one darn difference. She could feel her way through the rhythm of a conversation, knew when it was over, but didn't know the first thing about vintages, vineyards, or varietals.

"You like it?" He asked, slipping his phone back in his pocket. "It's a 2011 IL BARONE

Reserve Cab from Napa. There's this amazing castle you can visit, seventeenth century style, have you been?"

Her hazel eyes reflected splashes of the bold red wine as she viewed him over her glass. "You live in a castle and your extracurricular activities include castle visits. I live in a small craftsman home where the hot water runs out after the first shower, and my extracurricular activities include figuring out how to play soccer so I can practice with my son in the park and pretend I know what I'm doing like all the dads do."

Her words snapped her back to reality. "I really do need to get home, as lovely as this has been."

"Archer is fine, you said he's with your mother, right? So he's fine. You should relax a little, Emerson."

"Never tell a woman who does it all to relax. You'll get the opposite effect." Images of perky and carefree society women filled her head in contradiction to her untidy, hectic life. "Well, depending on the woman, I suppose."

"You're a woman who has it all, you deserve the downtime that goes along with being snowed in."

"Having it all and doing it all are very different things." Temper nipped at her. "I do it all because I have to. My mom, I love her, but she's always been dependent on others—my dad, then me—and I don't ever want to be in that position. I do it all because I have to or it will fall apart. It isn't a choice for me, it's my life."

She wasn't the same adventurer he'd met in New Orleans. She had responsibility now, a rooted and steady life filled with family, and she wore it well. Generally he'd be firmly and freely focused on the ride of life and where it would take him next. But in the face of a woman who had what eluded him, what he craved in the face of his brother's illness and frequent trips to the hospital, was building a life with the woman who stood before him.

Puzzled by his own thoughts and deciding to see where they went next, he clasped her fingers with his, gently so she wouldn't resist, and held her hand to his lips to set a soft kiss on her heated skin.

"You're Superwoman."

The lines around her eyes burst as a quick smile lit her face. "Archer would appreciate the reference. Some days I feel like Superwoman, some days I feel like a measly moth struggling to get to some sort of light, to make things brighter and better somehow—business, my son's life, my mom's life."

"Your life," he added, guiding them toward the living room where the fire greeted with pops and sizzles.

"Giving my family a good life gives me a good life. I'm lucky for my job and they're lucky to have me. That affords me the ability to give my mom and Archer the life they deserve."

She'd nailed his thoughts about family, clearing up his own mind. He wanted a family, to give a family a good life. He helped his brother and sister and parents as much as they asked for it, and some extra they didn't ask for, but he wanted a unit of his own. To share a good life together.

"Are you happy?" He asked as he let go of her hand, passed his wine to her, then piled another log in the fireplace.

"Don't they make fireplaces where you don't need to use real wood? Wouldn't that be easier?"

The fire snapped and sparked with the latest addition of the log as Emerson and Liam settled on the worn cognac colored leather couch.

"Easy isn't something that's always interesting. Sometimes it is but not always. I built this place to be removed from the life in the city where people are always around to do things for you. I have help here but they keep up with the property more than any-thing. In the city, my time goes toward busi-ness and there's always someone around to drive, to order meals, to clean salt off my shoes in the winter. Here, I kick off my shoes by the door, no one touches them, and I bake my own damn cookies." He smiled, took his wine glass back from her, drank from it.

She watched him, cool shadows and warm light dancing on the sharp features of his face. "We really do have completely different lives. Did you live like this when I met you?"

"Nope. Worked at a start-up that was later bought so I got a nice payout, then made some lucky investments and it grew from there. My mother and father had a dry cleaning business in Boston. They ran it together, went to work together everyday, came home together every night. My broth-er and his wife took over when my parents retired, and my sister and her husband just franchised the business into three additional neighborhoods. I was sort of the wild card of the family who didn't follow in anyone's footsteps."

In business or in love, he thought.

"Do you want what they have? You sort of look like you might."

He reached for her hand again, found that it tucked easily into his.

"I can honestly say I have no interest in dry cleaning," he said, gray eyes gleaming.

"That's not what I'm asking, but okay. What's that look on your face, then, when you talk about your family?"

"You still haven't answered my question from earlier."

"What question?"

"I asked if you're happy."

"Yes, of course I'm happy," she set down her wine next to the drink he'd handed her earlier that she'd abandoned.

"Anything missing? Anything you'd change?"

"Fewer business trips would be nice."

"Very funny."

Her wide smile radiated the shimmering glow from the fire. "Present trip aside. Though I'm still mad at you about that, I would like to travel less. I feel like I'm missing important moments in Archer's life, you know? Even something as silly as cupcakes ...I'm missing making the memory with him as much as I'm missing making cupcakes with him. That sounds crazy, probably, to a man who visits castles and lives in one of his own."

"Doesn't sound crazy at all." He drank as he gathered his thoughts, decided on his words. "It sounds...meaningful."

Her heart warmed, soothing the tension that had bunched in her belly from talking about her son. Pleased he understood, curious about the streaks of sad in his eyes, she lifted his free arm and laid her head against his chest.

"It is meaningful. I love my life. It's tough, at times, feeling pulled between work and family, but I do the best I can. Sort of always failing in one way or another—either failing at my job or failing my son—but I do what I can to make up for it in ways that are, yes, meaningful, I guess."

His arm wrapped around her, resting across her shoulders. The warmth from the fire felt good, but not nearly as good as it felt to have her tucked into him.

Liam would admit to being curious about her, fascinated by the thought of her, wondering where she was and what she'd done with her life. He would admit to wanting sex with the beautiful redhead, the fiercely passionate woman, but he hadn't known how well she'd fit. Emerson slid into his life with the beauty, heart, and flame that was uniquely her.

She was what he wanted, what had been missing. He'd known the want within him; he just hadn't realized how deep it went.

Chapter 5

Emerson's fingers typed fast across the keyboard of her laptop responding to emails. She checked the status of her team's prioritized projects, fielded questions from partners, instructed her assistant to re-arrange her schedule.

She thought about checking on Liam's assistant and the cupcake order then decided to let it go and let it be handled.

Then she reconsidered and asked her own assistant to follow through even though it was a personal task. Mixing business and personal wasn't a regular practice but given the circumstances, she made the exception.

She opened a data file on her computer and pulled some numbers she wanted to check against her team's conclusions—she hated numbers so she was diligent about double-checking. Pulling her legs up to stretch down the length of the couch, she crossed her feet at her ankles and dove into work as she usually did in the evenings after Archer went to sleep.

It was early still, but hard to tell time away from the schedule and routines with her family.

Glancing up to the high windows, only inky black could be seen with swirling white flakes making it look like it was raining stars. Night had arrived as fast as the storm and, with a heavy dose of guilt, her insides tugged between wanting to slow down the evening, to seep in the experience, and wanting to speed it up so she could get home and back to her purposeful life.

Time would tick away as it always did and she didn't need to worry about it, she reminded herself as she got back to work.

Occasional clanks came from the kitchen, echoing down the stone hallway from where Liam made dinner. Scents of marinade meandered along with an oath and a gruff dog bark here and there.

They were happy sounds, homely sounds. Looking up from her computer again, she wondered what it was like to live in such a grand and expansive castle. It should have been cold, dark, and empty given that one man lived alone in it. But it wasn't. Somehow it managed to be fun, warm, insularly cozy, and comfortable despite the winter storm that pounded outside.

At least enemies weren't pounding outside the walls of the castle, she mused.

And she knew, despite being snowed in against her desires, that she was exactly that—comfortable.

Not that Emerson wanted to notice any of this. She had her own home, her own family to be thinking about. Relaxing into the life she was snowed into was dangerous and guilt-ridden.

She sipped from her wine glass and reminded herself she didn't need to feel guilty; it wasn't her fault she was stuck in New Hampshire while her son and mom were in California.

It was Liam Wyatt's fault.

Back in a work zone, she fired off a detailed response to a restless client she considered high-touch. Likely not worth the revenue if one were to subtract the amount of time spent handholding, but the bottom line looked better and she'd gotten a gold star and a nice bonus. Payment for biting her tongue and exercising patience, the way she figured it.

And she thanked God for the payment as neither silence nor patience were strengths of hers.

When a bell rang through the castle, re-verberating off of the tall slabs of stone, she was reminded of where she was—very far from home. Her own doorbell had been broken for the last few months and fea-tured a pitiful sound that did more gurgling than ringing. Archer had volunteered that it sounded like a cat in a blender being blend-ed in slow motion. The kid wasn't lacking for imagination.

As she heard voices echo, Emerson smoothed a hand over her mane of red out of habit and hoped she looked presentable.

Then a small glimmer of hope shined—if they got in, she could get out.

But hope dimmed at the duet of women's laughter and talk of power outages and road closures that trailed in from down the hall.

Moments ticked by while she waited for them to enter the room.

"When I was in Tuscany last spring there was nothing, I mean nothing, that came close to the utter regality of this place you have—"

Still clad in Liam's white collar shirt and the large wool socks covering her feet that were kicked up on the couch, she struggled to not let her back stiffen at the sight—and smell—of the women who'd clearly made an effort to pretty themselves up.

Liam scratched at the stubble on his chin as he led the additions into the room.

"Emerson, this is Grace who has a house across the way, and her niece Hannah. Their power is out so they bravely schlepped over and brought cookies they baked today."

"Chocolate chip, your favorite." Grace winked at Liam.

Emerson eyed both Hannah and Grace's freshly coiffed golden hair, the swipe of glossy lipstick, the long, curled lashes, and decided whatever their game was, she wanted no part in it.

Power outage. Right.

She fixed a smile on her face she knew wouldn't last. "Nice to meet you both. You must be cold from the walk over. Come take my seat in front of the fire, I've still got some work to do. Excuse me."

As she gathered her computer and straightened the pillow, trying not to lean over and flash the New England debutante and regal aunt who were likely members of the Daughters of the American Revolution or Junior League or both, Liam strode in and set an arm around her shoulders. He was keeping her in place and she didn't care for it. She didn't have on any pants, dammit, and was feeling feistier by the minute.

"Emerson and I were just about to have another drink before dinner. Join us?"

She hissed through her clenched teeth.

As the smiling women sent sterling sparkles to Liam and daggers to her—a subtle difference perceivable by any observing woman—she fought to not get sucked into whatever game they were competing in.

If the prize was Liam Wyatt, they could have him. She was on the next plane out anyway, she reminded herself.

Her back still went up. Out of reflex she decided, nothing more.

"Poor thing doesn't even have proper clothes!" Grace announced with the sweetness of a sugar cube then muttered, overtly, to Hannah. "She must be from the shelter in town. Liam supports a whole manor of charities and charity cases."

"Excuse me?" Emerson demanded, mad that she'd been thrust into engagement and still wasn't wearing any damn pants. "I'm not from a shelter, nor are my living arrangements any of your business."

"Wine for you ladies?" Liam interrupted the baring of claws before the scratches started. "We've opened a cabernet if that works for you. Two glasses?" He started toward the wet bar in the room.

Emerson glared but gave points to Liam for saying "we."

"Hannah loves a good glass of wine. Not hours ago, she mentioned wanting to go on a chateau wine tour in France. Oh I just knew you two would have a lot to talk about." Grace exclaimed, pulling her attention from Emerson and apparently deciding she no longer existed.

Rolling her eyes, Emerson left the room without announcement.

As she reached the end of a hallway, she cursed the idea that her admittedly dirty clothes were still crumpled in the kitchen. There had to be another path that didn't involve walking back through the living room the vipers were in. Even if her shirt was covered in paw prints and lipstick, it was an improvement over what looked more like a nightshirt.

Or an after-sex shirt.

Not that she'd mind waltzing by with her clothes in hand, but she didn't need to play that game—she had a life, a family, a child. She didn't need to compete for a man she'd already had sex with. A fling. One didn't need to compete for a fling. The fling was over anyway, so she didn't care.

Sort of didn't care, she corrected, as she pulled open door after door looking for another path, something, anything to spare her the walk of shame through the castle.

When she pulled open the door to a closet the size of her living room, she stared. Around the room were stacks piled high and racks crammed full of clothes. When she spotted the obviously female section her stomach dropped.

"You better not be married, asshole."

Realizing his neighbor, the ungracious Grace, would know if he was married, and the obvious flaunting of her niece signaled otherwise.

She set her laptop on a nearby table then checked the rack of cashmere sweaters in a selection of colors and sizes.

"Okay, so...you, what? You're a playboy who has a room for people you bring here and who forget their clothes?"

Finding her size in a heather gray V-neck cashmere sweater, she tugged it off the rack with little trepidation, letting the hanger rattle on the rack.

Flustered, she flipped through the pile of jeans neatly folded on the stack of shelves and pulled out a pair of skinny Hudson jeans in her size.

She frowned as she looked at herself in the full-length mirror. It was a good thing she wasn't competing because next to the debutante, she looked downright shaggy. She'd flown all morning, endured the horrors of a helicopter, had fainted when she reached ground, had slept through the beginning of a major snowstorm, and had had sweaty, invigorating sex with a man who knew how to handle a woman.

God, did he know how to handle a woman, she thought, the knots in her stomach loosening.

Well, it wouldn't hurt to make a little bit of an effort to look acceptable...

She ran her fingers through her hair to smooth, pinched at her cheeks for some natural blush, and rolled her shoulders back.

Passable but not at all interesting.

Itchy with herself all of a sudden, she clicked through a rack of more clothes, eyeing each piece with increasing discrimination. As she pushed past a periwinkle James Perse T, her eye caught a glimpse of the long-sleeved royal blue maxi dress.

Exactly the right size, she noted. Wrong season for a dress, but what did she care at this point? Well aware of the ridiculous competitive spirit that had reluctantly sparked, she tossed off the jeans and sweater and pulled on the dress that clung around her hips and boobs, and bunched on the ground. It was too long by a couple inches, but she'd keep on the wool socks and stay indoors so what did it matter? And the scoop neck covered just enough to not be slutty.

There, she thought. Now she was armed for battle with the oh-dear-my-power's-out damsels in distress.

It was a ridiculous game, and she knew it.

But, away from her son, away from professional responsibility, she felt the momentum of having a small and petty streak of fun and decided to go for it.

Doing a quick turn in front of the mirror and a fast jiggling lift of boobs—Marilyn Monroe style because she may as well have fun—she opened the door ready to perform. With a smile on her face, she strode back into the living room where voices lifted and echoed.

Fully committing to the moment, she walked straight for Liam, who sat in a high-backed leather chair, and leaned down, laid an easy kiss on his cheek.

"Sorry for the delay, everyone. What do you think of the wine?" Her voice interrupted.

Grace's face melted into antipathy while Hannah shyly scanned Emerson's figure.

"You look...fantastic." Liam ran his knuckles along the edge of his jaw covered in dark stubble.

"Thank you, darling." Emerson sat on the arm of Liam's chair, winked at the two ladies seated on the couch.

Liam pressed his lips together, biting back a grin. So, the lady had some spit in her. He figured he'd have to go retrieve her from her computer and convince her to join them. But instead, there she was, clad in a dress she'd likely found in the monster closet, ready to battle.

He didn't know if he should be honored or amused and figured a little bit of both were good for a man's ego.

Pleased to play along, he laid a hand casually on her leg. "Grace here was just telling me she'll host a fundraiser for my campaign."

Emerson caught herself before she asked what campaign he was talking about. This was why she never lasted long in mating games and preferred a direct approach—stories always crossed and became complicated.

"Grace, that's wonderfully kind of you. Cause to celebrate."

"Well," Grace said emphatically, "the state needs changes and Liam here is powerful and knows how to get the job done. Of course, you'll need a Jackie on your arm, you know, dear? Not a Marilyn—blond, brunette, red-headed, or otherwise."

Emerson brightened, not only at the Marilyn comparison—which was laughably inaccurate but something that had just been on her mind—but also because she saw the effect she was having. Any game that had her being compared to Marilyn Monroe was a fun one indeed.

"Funny you should bring that up, I was accepted to George Washington University where Jackie O attended. Their B-school is one of the best. Settled on Berkeley instead."

"What's B-school?" Hannah asked pertly.

"Business school, honey," Grace responded with hushed curtness. "You must forgive our Hannah. She's been in Florence studying great works of art and creating some of her own. She's a passionate woman, filled with life and desire." Grace ended on a flourish while Hannah silently and uncomfortably looked around the room.

"Understated passion," Grace amended. "She paints her passion so elegantly. You really should come see some of her paintings, Liam. Just wonderful; they lift my soul. You studied business then I assume?" A small smile fixed on Grace's face as she turned back to Emerson.

"I did indeed."

"It was Da Vinci, I believe, who said 'Intellectual passion drives out sensuality?'"

Emerson's temper flared. "Why yes he did. And he also said, 'Blinding ignorance does mislead us.'"

"Dinner's about ready," Liam rose before the women began to throw down—not that it wouldn't be entertaining to watch and his money was definitely on Emerson, but he needed Grace if he was going to run in the next gubernatorial race.

"Em, honey, why don't you help me in the kitchen. And, Grace, you know the way to the dining room. You and Hannah mosey that way and we'll get everything ready for you."

Grace stood, chest puffed, mouth stern with the lines of it pursed. "Of course, dear. I know the way around here just fine."

Liam reached for Emerson's hand, pulled her down another hallway toward the kitchen, passing the dog, Darwin, who ran in the opposite direction with a bone in his mouth.

Chapter 6

"What were you going to do next? Punch her?"

"She started it! Since she walked in the door she's been insulting me."

Liam faced Emerson, placed his hands on her shoulders. "Yes, she has. And you've been dishing it back."

"She deserved it."

"Yes, she did. You look incredible by the way. Darling."

Emerson huffed out a breath. "When I'm not so mad I'm going to ask you about that ridiculous closet you have back there."

"And when you ask, I'll tell you that last month I hosted my corporation's holiday party here and my assistant bought a room full of extra clothes, knowing most would drink too much and stay the night and need clothes the next day. She went crazy with my credit card and I've since dubbed it the 'monster closet.' At the time I thought she'd lost her mind but looking at you now in that dress, I'm inclined to thank her.

"So are you done insulting the senator's wife? Can we have a civil meal together?"

"The what?"

"Grace is Senator Van Morten's wife. I've been toying with the idea of running for Governor next term and Grace and her husband will be instrumental in the run if I go for it."

Deflated, Emerson shimmied out from under his hold and leaned back against the island. "I'm an idiot. I'm so sorry. Had I known, I...I'm an idiot. I didn't really mean for this to get out of hand. It wasn't really about the prize—you—I guess, but something playful kicked into gear and I wanted to...play. Stupid."

She let out a long sigh and her hands lay lax against her sides. "My temper got the best of me. I'm sorry."

Liam pulled the scalloped potatoes from the oven, set the dish on a towel on the counter then stepped toward her. "You fighting for me, Em, dear?"

She rolled her eyes. "Oh, knock it off. I just told you I don't care. I'm an idiot, and I'm sorry for that."

"You don't care about me?"

Her gaze lifted to his. It was too poignant, the way he asked, and it shook her. "You're free to do whatever you want to do, be with whomever you want to be with. I'm leaving tomorrow, Mother Nature willing, so I can't care. It's your life, you do what you want."

Liam's eyes darkened, glinting with flecks of light that snuck in and penetrated the smoke. "Don't move."

He pulled the prime rib out from the warming drawer, sliced a few thick pieces then tossed on a sprig of rosemary for garnish.

Carrying both the scallop potatoes and the steak away, he returned moments later.

She hadn't moved, not because he'd told her not to but because her mind was catching up to where her temper had flung her.

"I really am sorry, Liam. I'm not sorry for dishing it back to the senator's wife, she really did bring that on, but I'm sorry for not being the bigger person. I tell my son all the time that—"

His lips crushed against hers, heat and hunger combusting. Breath mixed with demand, the vivid spark and the shadowed dark.

"Take your clothes off," he muttered the order.

"What? No. Grace is liable to come in and accuse me of being your concubine. Plus, technically they're your clothes."

He caught her lips in a kiss, slow, seductive, and primal.

"Then I'll take them off." He knelt down, slid his hands up her legs, slowly, under the dress. His touch trailing, heat rising, her center pulsed alive.

Head spinning, she sucked in a gasp of air as his fingers found her wet and warm and wanting. The teasing, the sensation, the utter blaze that erupted under his touch flashed and sent her over into sensations that rippled through her, quivering her muscles.

His mouth found hers again, breathless and satisfied. "That was fast."

She opened her eyes and saw a grin tugging on his face. "It's been awhile."

"You're right. It's been at least an hour. Way too long."

"Years. Hours. Same thing." She reached out, cupped his face with her hands, pulled him toward her. "More please."

He pulled her, fast, into the nearest room with a door—a pantry with copper pots and containers of pasta, sugar, and flour filling the shelves.

"I've always wanted to have sex in a pantry," she said, tugging at the buttons on his shirt.

"I just want you." He pulled the length of the dress up and over her head then savored the softness of her skin along her neck in devastatingly gentle kisses. For all the speed and heat that dragged, demanded, restraint pulled him back, allowing for more attention, more potent focus.

She finished with his shirt and reached for the buttons of his jeans. "You say the best things."

Shivers of anticipation shook her body as she dragged the denim down his legs and felt for the hard warmth. "Now. I want you now."

Temptation, hot and ready, took over.

"One of these times I'm going to take it slow and devour you one bite at a time."

She lifted to her toes and planted a kiss on his lips. "Absolutely," she said then pulled him toward her until they reached the end of the narrow space and she turned around, glanced back over her shoulder. "But I want you now and you have guests liable to find us at any moment."

His hands, strong and competent felt around her hips, gripping, testing.

She reached back and guided him into her, slowly backing her body onto him while she pushed against the pantry shelf.

Her breath caught as he filled her. On a moan, he plunged again, then again, intently and overwhelmingly sliding with her, against her, in her.

Standing strong, holding onto her hips, he felt the sensations of her, slowly, until momentum took over and the fine thread of restraint broke.

"Oh God, yes."

He heard her whisper as her body tensed in tight pulses around him, clenching in places that pushed him over into oblivion with her.

Wrapping his arms around her, holding her close, their racing breath, their racing hearts, struggling to settle.

"You have the most incredible back. I got the better view here without a doubt." His lips skimmed along the back of her neck.

"My brain isn't working yet so I don't have a comeback. Pretend I said something witty or wonderful in response. That reminds me though, you have a lot of scars and a spray of little scabs on your arm, your side, your back. Sword fight? Gallantly defending the castle? I meant to ask you before but you send my brain into orbit with that body of yours. It's a skill."

She turned around to face him, lazy seduction teasing in her eyes.

"Our bodies play well together."

"Yes, yes they do." Her fingertips trailed over the marks on his shoulder.

"The scars are remnants of being a boy with a brother," he said, wariness drumming a sad rhythm in his head. "And the scabs are from the road-rash I collected a month or so ago on a hurried trip to Boston. Brother went into the hospital and I was trying to get down there as fast as I could. Laid down my motorcycle on the way."

"Oh my God, are you okay?"

His gaze drifted over her naked body, her petite figure with ample curves. "More than."

"That's scary. My son will never own a motorcycle."

"Good luck with that." He kissed the top of her head.

"And is your brother okay?"

This time he looked straight at her, his gray eyes translucent. "He will be."

Before she could ask any more questions, loud bells dinged through the castle.

"Please tell me you heard that too and it's not just in my head."

"Front door." He gave her perky butt a quick spank, bringing him back to the moment.

She laughed as she turned around then quieted when she heard voices.

Tugging on clothes, they each hurried and exchanged glances of sneaky conspirators.

"I probably look like I've been having sex," she said, wishing for a mirror before she re-entered the shark tank.

He took a look at her, skimmed over her hair, her face, down and up her body, then settled on her honeyed eyes. "You look like a satisfied and beautiful woman, Emerson."

Her heart raced at his direct sincerity, the way he looked at her, the way his presence enveloped her, and sent her senses spinning.

She'd have to remind herself of reality soon enough, she decided, so right now she'd enjoy the luxurious attention of an intensely attractive man for one winter night.

Chapter 7

The fluid laughter of women filled the windowless stone cocoon of a dining room. Sounds were amplified, scents of meat and potatoes wound through the air, and glowing light shimmered from inside the bold iron chandelier.

"Liam!" A trio of more blondes that had joined around the table greeted the only man in the room with a chorus of excited sentiment.

Emerson watched as Liam welcomed the obviously related ladies—their platinum hair and sky blue eyes gave away their relation in an instant. The Getty sisters, as they were introduced, cheerfully greeted her and settled into conversations that crossed over one another.

Refusing to feel out of place around a table of exquisitely glamorous women who each looked as though they belonged in the pages of a magazine—even Grace with her pointy fangs looked ready for a photo shoot—Emerson restrained herself to a position of listening and observing.

She figured the good news about the latest additions of women meant Grace was no longer locked onto her. Either she'd been dismissed as a threat, which was entirely likely, or the targets had been split.

Whatever the reason, she was ready to eat a hot and hearty meal. She'd worked up an appetite, she though with a small and sneaky smile. No, they'd worked up an appetite.

As far as she was concerned, her feisty spirit had taken her over the line of friendly competition—what else was new—but from her perspective, she'd won. She'd gotten great sex with a phenomenal lover.

She frowned at the word that crept into her. Lover. Was that what he was? He did have a presence, a depth, a sadness to him that made her want to connect with him and share her heart, her love, her energy with him. There was a connection, wasn't there?

No, there couldn't be. It was just sex. The evening would end soon enough, morning would come, and she would be on her way home to her family.

Making the best of it, she exhaled and glanced around the room.

The Getty sisters—Evelyn, Genevieve, and Caroline—explained their attempt to make dinner in the dark as their power had gone off, then, deciding to see what Liam was up to, they trekked through the cold to come to the castle they'd nicknamed "Camp Castle."

Happy to hear the women weren't there for some sort of orgy that Liam had covertly orchestrated—which had entered her imaginative mind—she comfortably dove into the conversation.

"Why do you call this place a camp?" Emerson asked. "I must admit, I pictured tent cabins."

"You're definitely not a New Englander." Evelyn's face bounced into a youthful smile. "Camp, here, is a glorified vacation house. Not everyone uses the term. Just the fun people."

"And we're fun people," Genevieve added.

"The funnerest!" Evelyn exclaimed then lifted a defiant shoulder. "I make up words when I drink wine. So what? I'm fun."

Liam's smile was a genuine reaction to the company, the layered laughter, as he looked around the table.

He thought of his brother tucked into the hospital bed, beeps and tubes around him. It wasn't fair and it wasn't right.

Spending days and nights in the hospital with him wasn't enough—Liam's insides kicked and screamed to do more but he'd been flattened by helplessness. He'd come back to the castle to take a break, to clear his head. To see Emerson.

"I'm a lucky man, tonight."

His gaze settled on Emerson as he spoke. Her flowing mane of red surrounded a daintily featured face that watched him—the feisty upturned nose, expressive blush in her perky cheeks, generous lips that accompanied her generous spirit, and wide, warm tawny eyes that turned colors every time he looked at them.

"The storm made me a lucky man."

"Honey, any night of the week you're lucky," Grace reached over and gave his hand a squeeze.

He agreed. He'd had a decent amount of luck, hard work, and opportunity in his life. But he'd spent so much time in the hospital with his brother lately that the cheerful smiles and buoyant conversations now before him had his heart feeling full. Fuller than it ever had been, he realized. The chaos he faced with his brother had carved a crevice, slashing dark and deep in him, and this unexpected night had filled in the shadowy canyons with light and laughter. And Emerson, with her grounded, fiery, and practical expressiveness brought heat that spread into the darkest of spots, soothing, comforting.

"So 'camp' is a term for a vacation house for fun and lucky people. I like it," Emerson said.

"As a kid, we spent summer weekends here in a little house on the west side of the property." He hadn't wanted to speak about his childhood—it cut too close to emotion. But the memory was there, just under the surface. "A woman rents the place now, she's ninety and stable and stoic as they come."

"Oh, how is Annie?" Caroline interjected.

Liam nodded. "Good, same. Flying south next month. Too many winters here, she said. Going to move in with her son in Flori-da somewhere, live year-round in warmth.

"Anyway, our old place has two tiny bed-rooms so my brother, sister, and I would usually camp outside in a tent we'd talked our parents into buying for us. It was cam-ouflage, so we all thought we were so cool and invisible in the forest. I always said that when I grew up, I'd build a camp big enough for the whole family. What I pictured wasn't too far off from what you imagined," he explained to Emerson. "But I could afford something bigger by the time I was ready to build, something with indoor plumbing, but the idea is the same. Something big enough for family to visit and have their own space. But it's still camp to me."

"This place is big enough to fit a family of two-hundred," Genevieve offered.

Grateful to leave his own nostalgia be-hind, Liam listened as the sisters launched into tales of their childhood summers spent in New Hampshire. Then layered upon those stories were Grace and Hannah's anecdotes from extended family vacations to Europe.

Emerson had to admit she was intrigued and decided to sit back and enjoy the parade of ladies in the "Camp Castle" of Liam Wyatt, eligible bachelor.

It was a good thing the sex had relaxed her, she thought as she followed a bite of meat with a drink of dry cabernet. Sitting back and enjoying wasn't usually part of her everyday. Then again, neither was sex. Usually she inhaled her dinner then tackled ten things that needed tackling before tucking Archer into bed, reading him to sleep, then tackling ten more things before she could even think about sitting down with a glass of wine.

Under lashes dipped in curiosity, she watched Liam interact, keep stories about his personal life poignant and simple, and she softened as her heart rate slipped back into easy beats.

He'd said there was something softer about her since they'd seen each other last, but there was something gentler about him too. He'd been quietly potent in New Orleans, she remembered, and now she saw that it was rooted in something deeper, something more vital than before.

As all eyes around the table turned toward her, she realized she'd been submerged in her mind, distanced from the conversation around her. Silence followed and she glanced around, hoping for a clue as to what she'd missed.

"Emerson is a business development extraordinaire." Liam eyed her with a faint frown, apparently answering for her. "She works for a technology start-up that saw upwards of a hundred and fifty percent year-over-year growth, a lot of it attributed to Emerson and her team."

Her mind snapped to attention and she set down her wine. "How do you have that information? We're privately held and our numbers aren't shared with anyone."

"I'm not just anyone."

Though his statement had been sincere, there were chuckles and nods of proud affirmation.

Emerson kept her eyes trained on his. "That's confidential information that's only shared with a select few stakeholders inside the company, not people who are deemed special, as you imply."

On a silent oath and a sigh, she looked around the table at the raised, groomed eyebrows.

"I'm sorry, I really am. I apologize—I think I'm just punchy from a sleepless night followed by a long day of travel, and now being stranded away from my son."

She zeroed in on Grace, deciding she needed to distance herself from the political life of Liam Wyatt. She had feelings and she expressed them; political life wasn't for her—she couldn't even make it through a dinner without snapping.

"Liam has been kind, hospitable, and steadfast, given the circumstance of my being stuck in his castle thanks to the storm, and I imagine he'll make an excellent addition to public office," she said formally. "My punchiness shouldn't reflect on him."

Fighting the urge to slink off, find a guestroom to snuggle into until morning, she reached for the wine bottle instead, topped off her glass.

"I think it's pretty courageous and selfless to run for office. I, for one, would never run. Bit of a temper from my mom's side," she explained.

"You've got quite the backbone young lady, and the fire. Perhaps you should go into politics," Grace declared.

Emerson eyed the woman, and when she gauged the sincerity level that accompanied the pressed grin, she relaxed her shoulders. "Politics and poker are not my games. If something's on my mind, it comes out one way or another. Seems to me politicians have to clamp down on their tongues more often than not."

Grace laughed, letting through a slight rasp intermixed with the pristine polish. "You're not wrong. But the good ones channel their efforts to make a positive change in the world around them, a passionate difference. Liam here's going to do exactly that."

"If I run. That's yet to be decided," Liam laid the silver fork and knife down on his empty plate.

"I'm actually surprised to hear all of this." Emerson said. "You live such a private life—there's nothing in the trades about you, no images, nothing. And yet, you're willing to put yourself out there for a very public life. Why?"

He studied Emerson, determined how much he wanted to share. "Bottom line is that I want to help people. There's only so much you can do to help when you're bumping up against the law in terms of public services, policies that are in place. I want to help in ways bigger than private and personal." He thought of his brother, of the maddening healthcare system, of the flux of people in need he saw pass through waiting rooms.

"Your bottom line is the foundation of a course for change that you, Liam Wyatt, are going to lead," Grace said stoically.

He reached for Grace's hand and gave it a companionable squeeze similar to the one she'd given him. "Let's leave it at that and keep politics for another evening."

He'd had enough. This was his one night he could think about happiness, not suffer-ing. About life, not the threats against it.

Acting on his request, Emerson changed the subject. "So what do you do, Caroline?" She rose and rounded the table, taking over as hostess, topping off glasses.

"I'm on the board of several non-profits. That's how I met Liam. I served as President of the local Boys and Girls Club and I convinced Liam to give us the money to build a rec center, which he did.

"That reminds me, Li, doll, you should come see the shiny plaque near the doorway with your name on it."

Liam's face was quick to grimace. "That was to be an anonymous donation."

Caroline laughed and Emerson watched as the two exchanged familiar conversation.

The man never ceased to amaze—he was insanely private yet apparently had an open door to friends and neighbors. At least of the female variety. He was wealthy beyond belief and would work for pennies to push governmental policy to help people.

She'd been right in New Orleans to call him a mystery man. But he was more than that—he was a mystery man with a heart.

Frowning at the sudden unease, she tuned back in to Caroline who was teasing him.

"I just missed seeing that narrowed scowl of yours when we try to give you honors or awards. It's been too long. You haven't been around much lately."

As the doorbell chimed through the castle once again, Emerson handed the wine to Liam and excused herself to answer the door since she was already standing.

Getting lost only once along the way, she considered her sense of direction improving, and the break from her confusing thoughts a relief.

"And it's another beautiful woman," Emerson announced cheerfully and sincerely, holding open the thick wooden door.

Behind the woman, millions of icy diamonds sparkled, lights of the castle reflecting on frozen white fields.

"Please come in. It's not letting up much out there is it?"

The brunette, red-nosed and curious, brightened. "Not in the slightest. And thanks for the compliment, I guess it was?"

"It was a compliment," Emerson affirmed. "There seem to be a lot of beautiful women around here, each more gorgeous than the next. If you give me your coat, I'll hang it... somewhere."

The woman removed her many top layers, leaving a puddle of melted snow on the floor in the entry. "Well then I'll take the compliment. Especially given that I've just faced snow and cold and wind and death."

"Death?"

"It's possible I'm being dramatic but close enough."

"I like you already," Emerson decided. "I seem to have a flair for the dramatic this evening."

"Well then I like you too. And the coat closet is around the corner, down the hall on the right. New around here? You'll catch on quick. I got lost too when I started coming here. I'm Lorelei, by the way."

"Emerson," she replied simply, deciding it wasn't worth the effort to continue to be insulted by the gaggle of lovely women who all braved storm and, as it were dramatically described, death, to reach Liam Wyatt and his imposing castle.

What was it like in the summer when there wasn't the obstacle of blustering weather? Did herds of stunning women show up ready for orgies?

She didn't want to think about that, she decided. She was there for one night and would enjoy herself. Plus it was winter so what did she care about other seasons in a place she'd never return to?

"Am I interrupting a date?" Lorelei asked. "You look like you're biting back being annoyed that I'm here."

Emerson laughed as she held the dripping wet jacket, hat, and gloves. "I can't hide a damn thing. Some days I curse those Irish roots. But no, I'm not annoyed nor am I on a date. Though I am hoping you can answer something for me."

"Sure."

"Please don't take this the wrong way, it's a genuine question, but what are you doing here? Did Liam invite you? I'm only asking because I'm starting to feel like I'm the one intruding."

Lorelei pulled lip balm out of her pocket and swiped generously at her chapped and grinning lips. "Liam keeps few people close, but those in his circle he considers close, he loves to have them around and they know it and love it too. He's very generous, and some nights he eats dinner alone, and other nights ten of us will show up unannounced because we don't have anything else going on. But there's always food, always wine, always conversation. Personally, my power went out and I was bored out of my mind so I ventured over. Does that answer your question?"

Emerson leaned in, wrapped her arms around Lorelei in a quick hug. "Beyond. You don't know how much I appreciate it. I was beginning to think I was interrupting an orgy."

Lorelei's laugh was honest and full. "I wish I would've known that. I would've played along."

"Information is dangerous in your hands, I see." Emerson smiled, nodded toward the maze of hallways. "The others are in the dining room, sounds like you know the way so just follow the scent of wine and steak. I'll take care of your wet things and be behind you in a minute."

"Is that orgy talk?"

Emerson chuckled all the way to the walk-in coat closet.

The man was surrounded by gorgeous, fun women who simply showed up at his door in droves. The idea that she'd been caught up in a competitive game was com-ical now. She was a mother, a business woman, and her home was on the other side of the country. Plus, she was liking the women—they were each bright, silly, stoic, and they all seemed to adore him.

So what was she doing there? By the looks of it, Liam could have any woman he wanted around and had them around with very little effort, if any at all. So why did he go to such effort to get her there?

He'd wanted her alone, and with each ring of doorbell, the space between them widened. But, he had to admit, he liked seeing her back up, watching as she handled herself, then adjusted and settled in. He liked watching the way she worked, how her mind took charge at times and at others flew off in a forward rush of emotion. She was questioning with flashes of spontaneity, responsible and decisive with streaks of passion.

Like her glimmering hazel eyes, the facets of her were never ending and constantly reflective of her thoughts. Her hair, an expressive show of passion, her skin, never keeping a secret hidden beneath the surface, her body, excitable and wild with sensuality. Everything about her was expressive and yet, he found himself on his toes about what would come out of her next.

He'd been with enough women to know how to keep things friendly, casual. Honesty worked well and he enjoyed the friendships that'd come from the occasional affair.

But something about Emerson had him wanting her—only her, and he wasn't feeling very casual. He wanted to hear her laugh, he wanted to feel her skin under his, he wanted her opinion on running for office, he wanted to share that he was scared shitless about the very real possibility his brother could die soon.

There was something raw about her—raw and ripe, unpolished and juicy with life—and as he saw Lorelei enter the dining room instead of Emerson, he put away his desires and disappointments for the moment and instead put his arms around the woman he'd almost married.

Chapter 8

"Where's Stephen tonight?" Liam asked as he poured a newly opened bottle of wine through an aerator into a decanter, then poured a glass for Lorelei.

"Stuck in New York, business trip. All the hotels were booked so I called your assistant, hope you don't mind. She got him in at one of your properties."

He handed her the dark glass of zinfandel he knew she liked, affably laid a warm hand on her shoulder, then returned to his seat. "Whatever works. Glad he got a place. I thought you guys were going to the Alps for a late honeymoon."

"Next week, if we can fly out of here." Lorelei sipped. "My favorite, fantastic, thank you. Genevieve, how are things at City Council? Heard you got in front of a certain bill about water rights. Nice work."

Liam held up a hand. "No politics tonight."

Lorelei's face gleamed in the lights. "Oh, that's right! Did you decide to run for Governor? Governor Wyatt. I like it. Nice ring to it."

"You must keep the Boys and Girls Club in the mix for your platform," Caroline added. "You've done a lot of work there, done a lot of good."

The women around the table murmured in agreement.

"Well thank you for you for your support, but that's enough for now. It's storming, we have wine, food—you hungry Lorelei?"

"No, thanks. I'm here for warmth and light and company. And wine." She purred into her glass.

A friendly grin pulled on his face. "You meet Emerson?"

Eyebrows wiggled. "New girl in town, eh?"

"Lives in California. But if I'm lucky, maybe she'll move here. Know where she disappeared to?"

"Putting away my coat. Plus she probably got lost. I keep telling you to give breadcrumbs to people upon arrival. So what's the story with her?"

All eyes landed on him.

"I like her. A lot."

Ooo's and aaah's and a whimsical whistle echoed in the room.

He shook his head, let out a laugh.

"Well this is quite the development. Liam Wyatt declaring he likes someone. A lot. Never heard such a thing from you."

"Not true. I like each and every one of you."

"You know what I mean," Lorelei said, knowing that'd he'd once liked her a lot too. Just not love, she thought without sadness. It hadn't been love for her either—and she was madly in love with her husband now.

"So tell us what it is that you like about her. Quick before she gets back in here. We want the scoop."

"I'd tell you you're all hopeless and to mind your own business but you outnumber me at this point." His smile faded as he thought through his words. "I don't know how to describe it. It's like... It's like I know her, have known her for ages, and yet I just met her and can't wait to get to know her. That makes no sense."

The teasing stopped and the women listened with care and protection over the man they considered one of their own.

"That's the most lovely thing I've heard in a long time. Are you in love, honey?" Grace asked as a mother might.

He took a deep breath, exhaled. "I don't know. But I want to find out the answer to that with her."

Possibilities lulled the room into wistful silence.

"Unless she fell through a trap door and into the dungeon on her way back from the coat closet," Hannah's soft voice teased.

"Well no one here's allowed to push her in the dungeon. She's had a rough day already." Liam's gaze zeroed in on the woman who'd seated herself at the head of the table. "Grace."

She lifted both palms into the air. "Had no idea how you felt, darling. I'm a schooled woman now and your heart is important to me, just as your head is. Need both to get you into office and keep you there, the way I see it."

"As I said, I'm a lucky man."

"You are that. Plus I don't think she'd appreciate you protecting her like a king protecting his queen. I get the sense she can handle herself."

Pride warmed him at the idea that Emerson's strength was seen by Grace, a woman he considered to have resolve of steel. "You're right about that."

"How does anyone survive the labyrinth of hallways around here?" Emerson asked as she burst into the room. "I can't tell you how many ridiculous doors I've pushed through. You have a nice library, by the way. Found that on accident. Also, Darwin the dog seems to have his own playroom that's bigger than my entire house. I was starting to feel sorry for him, wandering around by himself, but he's in doggy heaven in there."

She paused, glanced around the room. "Why is everyone staring at me? Do I have spider webs in my hair or something?"

"Actually, yes." Liam walked to her before she sat, gently lifted a few stray strands of web from her face, then found her fingers and intertwined them with his. "Brandy in front of the fire?"

He felt Emerson's hand pull from his but he held tight, warm palm to warm palm. "Lorelei, you know your way around the bar; pour for everyone? We'll be right in."

"Great, what'd I do now? Ruin your chances of one day running for President or something?" She asked once they were alone.

His lips found hers before she could continue talking. The shared heat, mouths meeting, tongues touching, pulled them both in. Bodies pressed together silently while the sounds of life echoed down the hallway.

"Well," she said, catching her breath, "that was quite a kiss, Mister President."

"You're quite the woman."

"And you held my hand in front of your parade of women. What was that all about? Need rescuing? I'm happy to play along."

He caught her lips, hovered, nipped again, then deepened the kiss into something else entirely. Something not at all playful, but something that spoke of more.

"No playing. I like you, Emerson. I want to know you, more of you." He ignored her reference to the other women, focused only on her, and felt her breath hitch against him.

"I...Well, I guess I'm here until tomorrow so ask whatever you'd like if you want to get to know me." She let out a breath. "That sounds stupid compared to what you just said. I just...I don't really know what to say."

His eyes that had gone a silvery gray studied her. "I've never met anyone so immediately expressive. You fascinate me."

Her face pulled into a dismissive scowl. "I'm not fascinating, I've just got Irish in my blood. We're an expressive lot."

Lips lingered close, breath mingled. "I like that about you. A lot."

Alone in the dining room, the long table stretched before them, desire humming between them.

"You have guests," she pointed out, watching his mind consider the table, consider her.

"They can entertain themselves," he decided as he picked her up, set her on the end of the thick plank of wood.

Chapter 9

"**W**ho knew sex was so powerful?" Breath racing to calm, their laughter lingered in the dark dining room.

"We combusted and killed the electricity. Completely worth it," he responded and fastened the last of the buttons on his jeans.

Working to straighten clothes and hair in the pitch-black room, neither said a word. Emerson took the still moments to find her voice, to speak the questions on her mind as thoughts returned. "Why did you bring me here? You clearly have your pick of women if all you want is sex. Actually you have your pick of women regardless of what you want. So why go to all the trouble?"

Because she couldn't see his face, she couldn't judge his silence. In negotiations with business partners, silence was potent and open for interpretation. But in the dark, there was nothing to read, nothing to perceive.

She stood still, ready to return to the others who were likely huddled around the fireplace for warmth and light, and found the quiet unsettling by comparison.

"I have a different answer now than I did when I sent for you."

Irritation breathed on her neck making her inner independence twitch. "This is the twenty-first century. You don't send for women. You did however trick me into coming here under false pretenses which is completely different than sending for someone."

She exhaled at his silence.

"You really are quick on the trigger, aren't you?"

"You can evaluate my shots after you've answered the question."

"Feisty," he stated with a hint of a smile in his voice. "I like it. And I like you, Emerson."

She waited for more, and when none came, she offered sarcasm, "Well, that explains it."

"I wasn't finished yet. Are you always this impatient?"

"Yes."

"Ah."

"I have a lot to juggle in my life and my productivity is directly correlated to my ability to be impatient enough to cut through the crap."

"You think what I'm saying is crap?"

"I wouldn't know, you haven't said much." She heard herself, she heard her tone and, given that it was impossible to see one another, she took the moment to roll her eyes at herself.

He exhaled into the silent darkness—annoyed with and appreciating her snappy impatience.

"When I met you in New Orleans years ago, you were full of life and passion and your presence stuck with me. I've carried it with me, and every now and then it sneaks up and I think of you. I love adventure, I loved that you were so adventurous and vivacious. I thought of you then saw your picture in the trades and figured it was my second chance.

"I brought you here because I wanted adventure. But..." He pulled in a deep inhale then let it out. "I find myself wanting you to stay because I like you."

His hand reached hers in the dark and startled her, her pulse dancing under his grip in response.

"I like you and I want to know more of you. I want to know if you're stubborn for the sake of it, or if you're just used to doing everything on your own. I want to know what you're like when you're in love." He swallowed hard at his use of the foreign word. "I want to know what's in your heart."

Spinning like a dervish, her mind grabbed for words. "Have you? Ever been in love?"

He pulled her in to tuck against him. "I've cared deeply for women I've been with but mostly it's just been adventure."

Bodies pressed together in the dark, the quiet in the castle dining room, the cool whispers of air surrounding, and the heat of each other warming.

"My brother is going to have surgery again soon." He continued. "Just waiting for the call on the date and time." Liam's steady voice shook and he took a moment to calm.

"His wife's been by his side every step of the way. And it's... I don't know, beautiful, I guess, that they have each other. And that's been missing for me, in my life. It's been missing and I thought of you. So I brought you here. Tricked you. Whatever you want to call it. I just wanted to see you.

"You're a spirited woman with a beautiful heart, Emerson Brown, and I like you."

Chapter 10

The bronzed glow from the fire offered a heated halo around the guests in the living room while shadows danced on the fringes of the darkness, wiggling in the drafty tugs of air.

Between the stories told while huddled around the fireplace, Liam's phone dinged through the dark. He lifted it from his pocket, read the message, then went back to holding Emerson's hand, this time clasping a bit tighter.

Evelyn and Genevieve were busy grilling Hannah about cafes and bars in Florence, of which Hannah hadn't visited a single one while she'd been there, and Grace, Lorelei, and Caroline reviewed everything from the highlights of the latest town council meeting to Lorelei and Stephen's upcoming honeymoon plans.

Murmured conversations, a hissing fire, and Emerson by his side were exactly what he needed. He'd read the update from his brother on his phone and the anxiety had clawed at him, fingers digging into his fear, threatening to rip it wide open. And there wasn't a damn thing he could do to fix anything, and that was maddening.

He tried to refocus on the moment, the cheerful chats, the warmth, but that claw was clenching his throat.

Fidgety and needing some cool air, Liam lifted Emerson's hand to his mouth for a quick kiss then stood. "I'm going to bring up more wood for the fire from the dungeon. Help yourself to more brandy."

"Need any help?" She offered.

He shook his head. "I'll be right back." Liam walked away from the circle of cozy conversation and entered the blackness by himself, using only the light of his phone to lead the way.

"The dungeon's a scary, scary place. Even scarier with the power out." Lorelei told Emerson. "It's no joke down there."

"An actual dungeon? I thought he was kidding. My son would go crazy to see a real life dungeon."

"You have a son? Stephen, my husband, and I want to have kids soon. Oh, a son! What's it like?"

Emerson wondered what Archer was doing right then, wished she could nestle her face against his, hear him gripe and giggle as she kissed him noisily.

"Archer is my everything. He looks at me like I'm his everything, like I have all the answers, like I can fix anything, and some days he looks at me like I'm the Joker to his Batman." She chuckled through the fast feeling of nostalgia that crept up. "He's into superheroes lately, which, of course, means I am too."

"Aww," the Getty sisters all chimed in a chorus, as they were prone to doing.

"That's it. I want one. Son or daughter, I don't care," Lorelei stated. "When Stephen gets back, that's what we're doing. Who can wait for a honeymoon?"

Grace cleared her throat before the conversation turned to sex. She had some things she wanted to learn about this woman, Emerson, if she was going to be in Liam's life.

"I have an idea," she said, taking over conversations of the court. "My father was a mathematician and we had this game we'd play whenever we had a new person join one of our famous dinner parties. It's called x plus y equals u."

"Math is not my friend," Emerson readily admitted.

"Then you'll like this. It's combining unknowns to get to know you. So 'x' is what you give us, top-level general things about yourself to get started, then we combine that with 'y,' which is each of us asking you a question, and then the sum of those things equals who 'u' are. Okay, five things about yourself—quick bits, honey. Go."

Emerson pushed away some stray strands of unruly hair that'd fallen in her face. Her back to the fire, literally and figuratively, the flames lit the edges of her hair making her look like a fiery queen.

A fiery queen who twitched and straightened then slouched, unable to figure a way out of the little game.

"Is that story true about your father and dinner parties or are you just wanting to ask me questions?"

"Both." Grace's dignified face grinned.

"Okay, fine, let's see. Uh...One, I have a son named Archer who has red hair, same as me, and is quick to express himself, same as me. Two, my mom is much the same and she lives with us. She's with him right now," she explained. "Home is California, that's three. In the bay area."

She considered, mulled over what would be interesting to the group of interesting women then settled on simple and top of mind. "Well, I hate traveling, makes me sick to my stomach. I used to tolerate it okay enough, but now it's just a pain. Would rather be home with my kid, which is never something I thought I'd hear myself say.

"So...one more. I...well, I guess I'll be overly honest and say that being around all of you is fantastic and also sort of uncomfortable for me. I don't have time for girlfriends and I work mostly with men so I'm out of practice. Plus, I've never really been a 'pretty one,' you know? You're all 'pretty ones' and it's intimidating."

Emerson smiled warmly at the group. "Alright! Made it through. I kicked math's ass."

"Emerson." Grace said only her name.

"Oh, sorry. I'm usually so good about watching my language or my son would instantly start repeating it."

"Curse away, dear. I'm just reminding you that you haven't finished kicking math's ass. We're not done yet, only with the first part of the equation—the x part. Still have y to go.

"And you are a 'pretty one' by the way, so stop thinking otherwise, it's contrary to your character."

"Coming from you, Grace, that's quite a compliment." Emerson said touched, then sighed. "Okay, let's get this over with. Who's first?"

"Are you in love with Liam?" Evelyn asked immediately then balked at the elbows that lodged into her sides. "What? It's what we all want to know."

Emerson laughed through the uncomfortable little prickles that perked to life on her skin. "He'd be the one I'd tell, wouldn't he? No offense to you, of course."

"That's pretty much what he said," Evelyn offered then squealed at another jab to her side.

"What he said?" Emerson's eyes had gone wide. "What do you mean? What did he say?"

"You'll get to ask questions soon enough," Grace said, sidestepping the matter.

"I'll go next," Hannah's quiet voice said. "I studied art in school so my question is, what's your favorite color?"

Because neither the Getty sisters nor Lorelei knew her very well, they gave her a pass on the softball question.

"Red, obviously." Emerson fluffed at her hair as the women laughed.

"How long have you and Liam been dating?" Genevieve jumped in.

"We're not. That was easy."

"No way, uh-uh," Lorelei wagged her finger. "You're not getting away with it that easily."

"She asked a question, I answered. That's completely fair," Emerson pointed out. "So what's your question?"

Lorelei scowled mockingly and considered.

"I have one," Caroline said with her long-finger pointing in the air. "Hypothetical. If you fell in love with a man who happened to own a castle, again, hypothetical," she repeated at the sidelong look she garnered from Emerson. "If you were, and you moved into said castle, would you invite over the circle of women who you first met in the castle for sleepovers and pie parties and wine in front of fires on cold winter nights?"

Emerson liked Caroline—beautiful, sly, and sweet. A good combo in a friend, she decided as the idea flashed through her. It did have a warm, fuzzy feeling to it. "Hypothetically, I think your idea sounds wonderful. I'd do exactly that in that fabulous, purely hypothetical world of yours. Yes."

Pausing from the game to peer toward the shadows Liam had disappeared into, she let herself, for one brief moment, linger in the thought of living there, in the castle. Archer running around with the dog, her mom making her famous twice-toasted peanut butter toast in the massive kitchen, her working with a view of the lake, just as Liam did. Evenings spent curled up on the couch in front of the fire with the man that made her insides melt with even the simplest of touches.

Grounding back into reality as the fire popped and hissed, she looked around at the women. "It is quite the fairytale here, isn't it? But then again, it's not my turn to ask the questions, however rhetorical. Who's next?"

"Is your job the perfect job for you?" Lorelei asked after careful scrutiny of the questions she wanted answers to. She was blissfully married now, and she wanted love for Liam. But, if she could be picky in her own mind, she wanted a woman for him who had a backbone, who wasn't lost in the dream of Liam, but rather the reality. Someone with the fortitude to live the fairytale in the real world. Someone who had her own purpose.

"I don't know that I'd call it the perfect job as I'm reporting to someone else which means I bite my tongue a lot. But the profession in general suits me. It uses both sides of my brain. Everyday is different—structuring different deals with different clients with different objectives. I like that. As much as I like the CEO I report to, I find myself holding back a lot of myself which could otherwise be channeled into the passion of my work, so that drives me a little nutty at times. I like it, love it even, and one day I'd like to have my own business to run so my passion can run free."

"Restraining yourself makes you feel held back," Lorelei said, understanding.

"Exactly. But I can't complain. I have a decent life and provide one for my family. In that regard, it is the perfect job for me."

A hollowed feeling snuck up. Her words were exactly right, and ones she could readily admit. But talking about her work, returning to her desk at her office, somehow felt...off. It was as if she'd gotten even bigger with her desires, with her feelings, and the thought of going back felt like she'd have to shrink herself down first before she could fit into her life again.

Odd, she thought. This had been quite the odd day.

"Grace, I believe you're the last question then I'll go find Liam while you ladies keep the game going."

"It can be a quick one," Grace said from the high-backed regal chair where she'd perched, listening, watching Emerson. "If your significant other was in public office, what would you see as the worst and best parts of that life, public life?"

An eyebrow shot up on Emerson's face. "That's quite the question, Grace. And I wouldn't expect anything less from you."

She sipped brandy from her glass that glowed amber in the firelight. "I think you all have the wrong idea about me and Liam. We knew each other years ago," she started, realizing she was comfortable sharing and no longer felt like she was surrounded by sharks but instead, women she could level with. "I mean, your hypothetical questions have been interesting but I go back to California tomorrow and it's almost assuredly going to be at least another handful of years before we see each other again, if ever at all." She swallowed another drink and frowned at the sudden lurch in her stomach.

"That doesn't sound very fun," Evelyn offered.

"No, it doesn't, does it?" After a deep breath, Emerson looked at Grace. "But to answer the hypothetical question—and yes,

I realize I'm talking to a woman whose husband is a senator, but I'm just going to be honest—the worst thing would be that I'd be expected to be smiling and pleasant on the sidelines all the time." She made a sour face. "I'm not good at that or interested in that. I'd do better with a purpose. And that would be the best part, I suppose. I'd use the power for bringing attention to children and the arts. My son is one of the most imaginative beings on the planet, and yet, public schools, at least in our area, fall short on the arts due to funding issues, budget cutbacks, and whatnot. I'd worry less about sending him off to school soon if there would be an outlet for his imagination, some way to help mold his strengths rather than ignore them or cast them off as not as important as other areas of study."

She stood, feeling passion and temper buzz in her fingertips, signaling she was antsy. "Anyway, I'll get off my hypothetical soapbox. Thank you all for the crazy game.

"Lorelei? Would you point me toward the dungeon?"

Grace watched as the pair walked off, silently nodding to herself. She'd heard exactly what she wanted to hear and felt better for it. Supporting Liam Wyatt in his run for office would be her next project and she was ready to get started. Now, all that was missing was Emerson of California standing next to him, strongly and with purpose.

She had confidence in Liam. The man would come to his own conclusions, she knew, as men did. Sometimes all they needed was a little matronly coddling and encouragement, and she'd see to that if necessary, but doubted it would be. The man knew his mind.

Chapter 11

She heard a whap followed by a cracking sound as she made her way down into the darkness. She imagined the stairs were covered with bits of brave moss and sticky puddles of dragon drool.

Emerson, of course, couldn't actually see the steps in order to judge what they looked like, but her imagination amused her on the blind trek downward into the dungeon.

She missed her son, she thought as her wool socks slipped a little on the step. They amused each other relentlessly and he'd be a fun little companion in the dark castle.

He'd be in his socks too, sliding around on purpose, sailing across the floors in his Superman cape.

The hammering crack sounded again, this time louder than the last.

"Liam?" Her voice echoed for seconds and her eyes widened as she wondered how big the dungeon actually was. "Jesus. I hope there isn't really a dragon down here that will flame me to death. Hopefully it's a magical dragon. Like Puff," she muttered to herself.

She heard the sound again and walked toward it.

"Liam? Please say that sound is coming from you."

"Over here."

The soft white glow from his phone spread around him as he appeared from behind a wall and walked toward her. "What're you doing down here?"

There was edge to his voice that hadn't been there before.

"You were gone for awhile so I came to see what you were doing. Also I couldn't take any more hypothetical questions. God, it's freezing down here."

"Why were you answering hypothetical questions to begin with?" He asked as he tugged her hand and walked her back toward where he'd been.

"Math," she said, as if that explained it all. "What're you doing down here? You seem. ..different."

"Stand there," he instructed. "And hold this toward me, like this." Liam handed his phone to Emerson, held it at the angle he wanted the light to shine, then walked off.

"Okay..." She said skeptically then jiggled in place to keep warm.

She eyed the dark, waiting, then she realized she and the white spotlight were alone. "So, I suppose I'll try asking again." Her voice lifted and echoed to reach wherever he'd disappeared to. "What are you—"

Her words were cut off by the sight of an axe flying from the blackness down onto a piece of wood.

"Holy shit. You could've warned me you were about to murder me."

"I'm not murdering you."

"You could've been. You should have warned me."

"What kind of murderer warns you before killing you?" He asked, tossing the kindling he'd cut off to the side in a clank.

"One with morals?"

Another thwack came down hard, more wood was split into pieces and she shuddered even though she was standing away from the action.

"A murderer with morals. Let me know if you find one."

"I'll start looking for one as soon as I make it out of here alive. Jesus." She pressed a hand to her pounding heart. "So, are you going to tell me what's going on? You really do seem..."

As another swing of axe broke through the thin light and shattered wood into smaller slices, she waited for the lull between blows, no longer bothered.

"Tense," she finished. "Or, angry maybe? I don't know you well enough to know which it is. But it's one of those."

"Neither," he said as he threw the wood onto the pile with more force than was necessary.

She waited a few moments, giving him space in the silence, in the darkness. "Okay, well, I guess I'll go back upstairs then. It's freezing down here anyway. I'll just set your phone right...here for you," she decided then laid it on the ground.

Emerson turned and walked a couple of steps, rubbed at her arms to warm them.

"Don't go."

She stopped walking, turned.

"Don't go." He tossed the axe into the woodpile and made his way toward her. He smelled of musky earth and fresh pine with hints of that masculine scent that was naturally his.

He approached and wrapped his arms around her, holding tightly.

Her head tucked against his chest, hearing his heartbeat pound steadily, her own pulse skipping along with it in response.

"My brother's going to have surgery tomorrow. It's experimental. I've been trying to fly a doctor in for a while to do it. That was my brother who texted me earlier, saying that it's been scheduled for tomorrow. So, the good news is you'll finally get out of here because even if I have to call in the National Guard, I'll be at the hospital in Boston tomorrow."

She heard that there was still a bite in his voice but at least she understood he was dealing, in his own way, with something that stung his insides. Family first, she knew, feeling very much the same.

"That's big news about your brother. I'm so sorry, must be difficult for all of you. What's going on with him?"

He breathed deep, exhaled. "I'll explain later, don't think I can hash over the details any more right now."

She held him just a little bit closer, a little bit tighter. "Your brother is fortunate to have you by his side. Even if it means you get road-rash along the way."

For suspended minutes, neither said anything and they stood in the dungeon with only the glow of his phone providing a haze of light nearby.

"I want you by my side," he said to her.

She pulled back, peered at him, the thick shadows casting razor sharp angles on his unshaven face, a harsh contrast of ferocity and vulnerability.

"I don't want anything to happen to him. He's my big brother and...I don't want to lose him. And I don't want to lose you.

I've lost you once, I don't want to lose you twice."

She tried to swallow but found she had nothing to actually swallow—her mouth had gone dry.

"My son. I can't keep staying away from him like this. It's not fair to him. Or my mom, she probably needs a break."

"Emerson." He said her name with gentle depth. "I'm asking you to stay with me. Be here with me. Maybe it'll work out with each other, maybe it won't. But I want you here for us to try. Say yes and we'll get your son and mother here tomorrow. We can send a plane for them, and yes, we can still make sure cupcakes get delivered to his daycare. He can even wear his Superman cape every day for all I care. Just...say yes."

She stepped back, touched that he'd remembered details like cupcakes and superhero capes that filled her head on a daily basis.

"What are you asking, Liam? You mean move in here with you? My mom lives with us too. I can't leave her in California."

Hearing her own words, she pulled in a thin inhale. She couldn't uproot her life to be so spontaneous. Especially for a man. She was an independent woman with a successful job and a healthy, happy son. She couldn't uproot their lives just to date a man.

Could she?

"Why?"

"Why?" He repeated her question.

"Why do you want me here? I mean, we barely know each other."

"Because from the moment I met you five years ago, I wanted to know more of you. You said you didn't want to exchange names, that we should be adventurous and spontaneous, and we said goodbye the next day. We did it your way then. But I want to do it my way this time. I want to know more of you. I want you and Archer to move here. Your mother too. She can take over the two-bedroom place on the property once Annie moves out if she wants her own space, or she can stay in here."

"I don't think my mom wants to live in a dungeon. Archer might."

He smiled and cupped her face in his hands. "I meant the castle, but wherever she wants. Hell, I'll build her a house if it means you'll move here."

She breathed deep, steady, and ordered herself to think as she felt her mind sinking into the possibility.

"But my job, my career."

"I love that your mind is practical at times and fiery at others. See, that's what I want to know more of. What's the trigger? What makes you choose one or the other? That's what I want to know.

"And you said yourself your boss is 'misleadingly intrigued' by me. He'll either let you work from here and be excited about the bragging rights of you working with

'Liam Wyatt, arrant butt-face,' or you leave there and come work with me."

"Unscrupulous, arrant butt-face," she reminded him.

"How could I forget?"

"Because you're unscrupulous," she tossed back. "So what if I want to start my own business?"

"Then start your own business. I don't think you understand. I just want you here, Emerson. The rest are just details to work out. Like you realizing I'm not an unscrupulous, arrant butt-face, for starters."

"This isn't funny. These are important details. My life details."

"I agree. And I want them to be our life details. Say yes."

She bit at her bottom lip, considered, and couldn't believe she was considering something so crazy and yet something that felt so right, so silly to make a big deal out of when it so easily snapped into place in her mind.

"I'll need to talk to them first, Archer and my mom, to make sure this is something they want too."

"Absolutely. Call them now."

She smiled. "You really are persistent when you set your mind to something, aren't you?"

"And so are you," he said and skimmed his thumb along her bottom lip where she'd bit at it.

"Yes, that's true. And," she pulled in a breath, held it, then exhaled. "Yes. I'll talk to them but I'm sure they'll both be fine with it once I explain the castle. Archer will immediately start jumping on the bed when he finds out—it's his current favorite activity with his cape on. And my mom would love it. She's Irish, and how can you be Irish and not have a fondness for castles?"

"I have a fondness for you, Emerson Brown."

She smiled just before he caught her lips in a kiss that heated her from the inside out, melting all the amazingly alive parts of her and sending sizzling sparkles of excitement to others. "And I have a fondness for you, Liam Wyatt."

She lifted to her toes as the kiss deepened with pleasure, with promise. "I'm sorry about your brother. Whenever you want to tell me more about it, I'd love to hear."

"Appreciate it."

"Anytime. So do you want to tell your harem upstairs that I'm moving in here or should I? There may be tears. Possibly some sharp objects thrown."

He laughed and grabbed his phone off the floor then took her hand in his, leading them toward the stairs back up.

"They'll love you because I love you. Eventually."

"You'll love me eventually?"

"Depends on how many sharp objects you throw."

She leaned her head against his shoulder, chuckled as they walked hand in hand. "Well that depends on whether or not you try to make me fly in that tin bug with top wings."

They reached the top of the stairs and started toward the glow of the fireplace once again but he stopped, faced her. "I mean that I love you. I never really knew what that meant, not really. But I want you to be happy, intensely happy, and I want us to be happy together. I want my brother to be okay. I want your family to enjoy living here. I want them to be my family too. That might be too much to ask, but it's what I want. And I'm really good at getting what I want."

She raised up again and met her mouth with his, feeling his lips warm beneath hers.

"Don't I know it?" She smiled, mulled over what he'd said. "I need time to let myself fall in love with you, Liam. I came here under fabricated pretenses and have been operating with the idea that I may never see you again after I leave. So I need time to let myself feel."

Her head shook and a frown burrowed. "Oh, who the hell am I kidding? I'm no one if I don't know what I'm feeling. I love you too. Dammit, Liam. I don't know if I believe in love at first sight."

"First sight was five years ago."

"I'm sure I could argue that point."

"I'm sure you could."

"But I won't because I like the sound of it."

This time he laughed as he held onto her once again, his arms wrapped around for security, for desire, for forever. If he got his way...

And he always did.